CHEESIE MACK

MACK

Is Not a Genius or Anything

CHEESIE MACK

Is Not a Genius or Anything

STEVE COTLER

Illustrated by Adam McCauley

random house New York

Text copyright © 2011 by Stephen L. Cotler
Jacket and interior illustrations copyright © 2011 by Adam McCauley

Visit us on the Web! www.randomhouse.com/kids

Educators and librarians, for a variety of teaching tools, visit us at www.randomhouse.com/teachers

Visit Cheesie at CheesieMack.com!

Library of Congress Cataloging-in-Publication Data
Cotler, Stephen L.
Cheesie Mack is not a genius or anything / Stephen L. Cotler ; illustrated by Adam McCauley.
— 1st ed.
p. cm. — (#1)
Summary: Ronald "Cheesie" Mack relates events he and his best friend, Georgie, experience as fifth grade comes to an end and their summer plans are drastically changed, due in part to an old, possibly valuable coin that may belong to the mysterious inhabitant of a place they call The Haunted Toad.
ISBN 978-0-375-86437-7 (trade) — ISBN 978-0-375-96437-4 (lib. bdg.) — ISBN 978-0-375-89570-8 (ebook)
[1. Friendship—Fiction. 2. Coins—Fiction. 3. Lost and found possessions—Fiction. 4. Conduct of life—Fiction. 5. Recluses—Fiction. 6. Family life—Massachusetts—Fiction. 7. Massachusetts—Fiction.] I. McCauley, Adam, ill. II. Title.
PZ7.C82862Che 2011
[Fic]—dc22
2009033329

Printed in the United States of America
10 9 8 7 6 5 4 3 2 1
First Edition

For all my grandchildren:

Ro
Cl
Th
Zo
Gr
Ma
Et
Rh
and
Mi + He

Contents

CHEESIE MACK

MACK

Is Not a Genius or Anything

Chapter 0
The Story Is Over!

This is the end of the book.

It was about a mysterious old coin, an evil sister (mine), a dead sister (not mine), runaway rodents, a super-best friend, a fifth-grade graduation disaster, some really unusual words (including a few I made up), and The Haunted Toad.

I wrote it. I'm Ronald Mack. People call me Cheesie. You can probably guess why.

I love mac 'n' cheese, but I almost never eat it anymore, because if I do, someone always says, "Cheesie Mack eats mac 'n' cheese!" And I've heard that two million times.

My name is in the title of this book because it's about stuff that happened to me, Cheesie Mack.

You probably noticed that this is Chapter 0. That's because I already wrote the whole story that comes after this. It begins in Chapter 1. I started writing a couple of days after fifth grade ended and have been at it nonstop ever since. And now I am writing this chapter last even though you're reading it first.

Everything in this book is true. I did not make anything up. I'm definitely not a genius or anything, but I remember all the details because I was there when everything happened. And if you're a kid like me who has adventures, there are going to be lots of details to remember. Details about stuff like:

1. Abraham Lincoln's head
2. The Point Battle
3. The Mouse Plot
4. Lawbreaking zoom chucklers

5. Ee-Gorg and Doctor Cheez

6. The letters *V*, *D*, and *B*

This adventure started the day before the last day of fifth grade. I hope you like it. If you don't or do or whatever, please go to my website and tell me.

Signed:

Ronald "Cheesie" Mack

Ronald "Cheesie" Mack (age 10 years and 10 months)
CheesieMack.com

Chapter 1
My Boring Graduation Ceremony

"I shall now scrape the burnt flesh," I said.

"Gross!" said my older sister, June.

We were in my backyard finishing dinner. My dad, my mom, and my grandfather were relaxing at the picnic table. I was cleaning the barbecue. That's one of my chores. Cleaning charred chicken chunks off the grill is greasy work, but I don't mind, especially if I can bug my sister while I do it.

I scraped the wire brush back and forth across the grill while sipping my second can of cream soda, which IMO does not taste a bit like cream.

"We should not cook anything that has a face," June said, piling dishes on a tray. She's a vegetarian. "So that means that we *could* cook you because the ugly blob on the top of your neck is definitely not a face."

My mother gave June a stop-it look, but June continued. "There are, however, those huge flappers sticking out from the side of the blob—"

"Enough!" Mom said.

Okay, so my ears stick out. I don't care. I won that one. One point for Cheesie. And that is the last time I am going to talk about my ears in this book.

My mother is an air-traffic controller. Her job is to keep track of airplanes and tell them where to fly. She works in the control tower at Logan Airport in Boston. She always brags that she can keep planes far enough apart so they don't crash into each other, but complains that she can't do the same with her kids. And when June and I fight, I usually get the worst of it because she's two years older and much bigger than me.

And meaner.

But I'm pretty sure I will be bigger than her when we're both in high school. I don't know if I will be meaner.

Mom walked over to the driveway, carrying a plate of meat and gristle and skin that she had torn off the leftover chicken bones. "Ronald's graduation ceremony begins at ten-thirty sharp tomorrow morning," she said, tossing the leftover chicken bits to my dog, Deeb, who is a very good jumper and midair scraps-grabber. "I don't want anyone to be late."

"When I was a boy," Dad said as I plopped down at the picnic table next to Granpa, "there was no such thing as fifth-grade graduation."

"When I was a boy," my grandfather added, "there was no such thing as fifth grade." He tried to poke me in the ribs, but I saw it coming and quickly slid away from him.

"When I was a boy . . . ," I said, pausing to take another sip of soda. But getting away from Granpa had moved me too close to my sister's cleanup work. She poked me much harder than Granpa ever would have, then scooted into the house grinning wickedly because no one saw her do it.

Drops of soda dribbled down my neck. One point for my sister.

I hooked my sneakers on the wood boards under the picnic table, leaned wa-a-ay back on the bench, and looked sideways at Dad and Granpa.

"When I was a boy, I—" But two cans of cream soda bubbles churning around inside me, along with the back bend stretching out my belly, wouldn't let me finish my sentence. I burped long and loud.

"Riddle-dee." That's exactly what it sounded like . . . sort of.

An instant later, my father rattled out a longer one.

"Riddle-dee-diddle."

Almost immediately Granpa topped us both.

"Riddle-dee-diddle-dee-dee."

We all sighed. "Ahhhhh!"

From the driveway, Mom shouted, "I heard that!"

"You're still the greatest, Pop," Dad said to Granpa.

"You should be in the opera," I told him.

We always say that to Granpa. He once burped the opening to "The Star-Spangled Banner." Musical burping is a Mack Family Tradition.

Mom thinks it's crude and rude.

Dad says she's a prude.

Granpa says it improves his mood.

I think it's dude.

It was the middle of June. Tomorrow morning I had to go to my boring fifth-grade graduation ceremony.

How did I know it would be boring? We had been rehearsing for three days, and here're all the boring things that we had to do for everyone's parents and grandparents:

1. Recite the Pledge of Allegiance. (Georgie Sinkoff, my best friend, said he was going to do it with his eyes crossed.)

2. Sing "This Land Is Your Land." (Georgie said he could hold his breath through the whole song—even while opening and closing his mouth like he was singing—and turn bright red.)

3. Sit quietly while our principal, Mrs.

Crespo, gives a speech. (The school nurse told Georgie it's about healthy eating habits, so he's going to pretend to throw up on Lana Shen, the girl sitting next to him.)

4. Listen to Francine Binki, who has perfect attendance, recite a poem she wrote called "Growing Up." (Georgie said he'll "grow down" by sliding out of his chair so slowly that no one will notice him moving at all. By the end of Francine's poem, he'll be totally out of sight.)

5. March up to the stage one at a time to get our diplomas. (When Alex Welch, who is last in our class alphabetically, walks past, Georgie said he is going to trip him because he is sure Alex is the kid who dog-pooped his bike seat.)

Georgie lots of times has terrific ideas, and if I'd maybe believed that he was going to do even *one* of these, I would have been happy to go. But there would be tons of grown-ups there, so I knew nothing would happen, and it would be very, very boring.

"I feel kinda sick," I said weakly, looking around at everything in the backyard except Mom, who had just sat down next to Dad. "I'm probably getting the flu."

"Cut the con job," Mom said. "You are *going* to graduation. My parents are driving up from New Haven, and there's no way you're—"

"Okay," I muttered, "just for Gumpy and Meemo."

I know those are really stupid names for grandparents, but don't blame me. My sister was born first. She made them up. But I invented Granpa's name. It used to be Grandpa, with a *d*, but when I was little, G-R-A-N-P-A was how I spelled it, and he liked it that way . . . which was surprising because Granpa disagrees with almost *everything*. He once told me, "If I don't get hot and contrary about something every single day, my blood'll probably just cool down, thicken up, and clot me to death."

The name Granpa isn't so rare, but I have never met anyone who has a Gumpy or a Meemo. I am collecting grandparent nicknames on my website, CheesieMack.com. You can put yours in if you want.

"I don't think Granpa can come to Ronnie's graduation," Dad said.

Mom looked at Granpa in disbelief. Granpa was looking up at the sky. She looked at Dad. He had his head down, pretending to brush crumbs off his fake foot. (When Dad was twenty, he was a sailor on a Navy aircraft carrier, and some guy dropped a bomb on his shoe. It didn't explode or anything, but it squashed his foot, so he straps on a fake one. It even has fake toenails.)

"Granpa's going to be busy," Dad finally said.

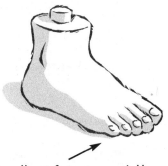

Excellent fake toenails!!

"There's too much red in my taillights."

I must have looked confused.

"Oh, yeah," Dad went on. "He'll be down at the garage draining the color."

My father owns four limousines. Those are very big and fancy cars. They're used for driving people places. He's the boss of his company. But he also drives the limos sometimes.

"Messy job. Probably take me all day," Granpa grumbled.

Mom got up and walked away without saying anything.

I knew they were kidding, so I squinted one eye shut and gave my father an evil pirate look . . . which he gave right back. Then I suddenly turned my head  and squinty-evil-eyed at Granpa, who instantly squinty-evil-eyed back at both of us. As you probably guessed, this is another Mack Family Tradition.  We probably would have kept squinty-evil-eyeing each other for a lot longer if the phone hadn't rung. My sister yelled from inside.

"Hey, Runt! Phone!"

I know her tricks. She gets no points if I ignore her. That's one of the rules of the Point Battle, which was 615 to 592. My sister was leading, but recently I've been gaining on her. I've been keeping track since the beginning of fourth grade.

So I walked into the house, paying no attention to

my sister and total attention to Deeb, who was running back and forth between my legs.

June almost never calls me Ronald or Ronnie or Ron. She mostly uses Runt, which I hate because I am actually the second-shortest kid in my class. Only Glenn Philips is smaller. And he has some kind of growth-hormone shortage in his brain that he's getting shots for. But he's also the smartest kid in the fifth grade and can tell you the names of all of Jupiter's larger moons. (I put a diagram here, but I included only the four largest moons because there isn't enough room for the rest. There's plenty of room in space, however.)

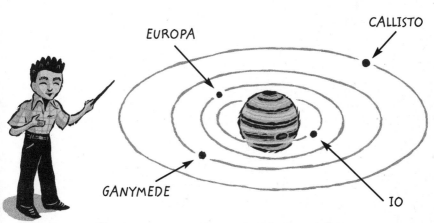

EUROPA

CALLISTO

GANYMEDE

IO

Glenn says there are over 60 moons, but even he doesn't know ALL their names.

"Runt!"

I hate when she does this. Probably one of my friends is calling, but if I answer her, she'll just smirk and say, "I see you finally know your real name."

I am a ten-year-old boy with big sister problems.

When my parents aren't around, I call her Goon. In my opinion, Goon is an excellent description of June's personality.

If I think up any new Goonish insults, they will be in my next book.

Chapter 2
My Best Friend Screams

The phone call was from Georgie Sinkoff, my best friend.

"GET OVER HERE RIGHT NOW!" he screamed into my ear before I could finish saying hello. And then he hung up on me.

I ran outside, yelled to Mom where I was going, and sprinted into the gully behind my house, which is in Gloucester, Massachusetts, where I have lived my whole life.

If you don't know where Massachusetts is, look in the upper right-hand corner of the United States. Turn the page for a map.

I left Alaska out because it's too big.

Mass (sometimes we call it that) is a small state.

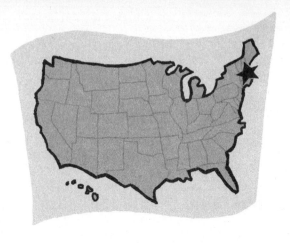

Only six states are smaller. Even Hawaii is bigger, but it's kind of cheating because lots of Hawaii is ocean. I have a U.S. map on my bedroom wall, and because I look at it every night before I turn out my light, I have almost memorized it.

Gloucester (people here say *GLAH-stah* . . . weird, huh?) is the oldest fishing port in America. It was founded in 1623, only three years after the Pilgrims landed at Plymouth Rock, which is also in Massachusetts somewhere. I have never seen Plymouth Rock, but rocks last almost forever, so I guess it's still there.

Georgie and I live less than a mile from the Atlantic Ocean, in a neighborhood of big, old houses. Not old like Pilgrims, but Granpa says our house is older than he is, and I know he is way more than seventy. (He does not celebrate his birthday, and I don't even know when it is. He won't tell.)

Our houses are three blocks apart if you use the streets, but Georgie and I only go that way if we're on our bikes. There's a scrawny little stream in a scrawny little gully that separates our backyards, and it is so narrow that last year Georgie launched a balloon filled with chocolate pudding all the way from his bedroom window over the trees and the gully into my backyard, where my sister was playing with her friends.

I told you he has terrific ideas!

Of course I was in Georgie's bedroom at the time, but on purpose here's what I *did not* do:

1. I did not fill the balloon with pudding.
2. I did not touch Georgie's huge slingshot.
3. I did not help pull back the rubber part.

I did not do any of these things so that if Mom or someone asked, I would not have to lie. I did help aim it, kind of. When the pudding bomb landed and splashed chocolate on you-know-who, the girls screamed like the universe was exploding—and even though we got yelled at, it was cool.

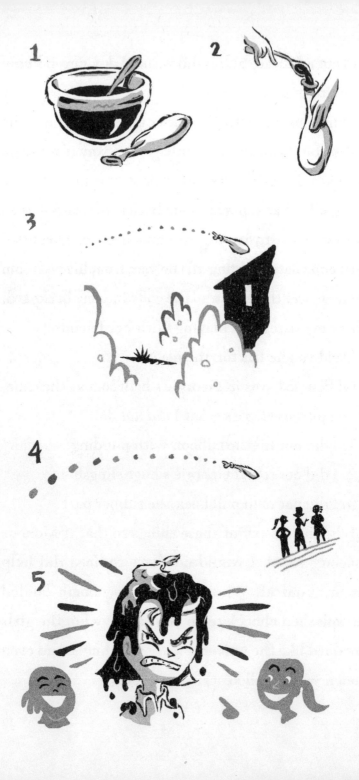

I trotted through the gully on the path that Georgie and I made, then up the other side and through the won't-close-gate into his backyard. Once inside his back door—I never have to knock—I yelled for him. He yelled back from the basement.

I walked down the stairs. They creaked and squeaked like in horror movies. (I'm not trying to scare you—it's just one of the details I remember.)

His house, like mine, is really old. The basement and stairs are made out of wood, and the floor is mostly dirt except for the concrete part where Mr. Sinkoff keeps his tools.

I could see a shadow moving on the basement floor, so I knew Georgie was directly beneath me, under the stairs. When I reached the bottom, Georgie stepped out and grabbed me, talking real fast.

"I found something big! Really big!"

There were cobwebs in his hair. He had one hand behind his back.

I have known Georgie my whole life. We have always been best friends . . . except for the time in third grade when he called me Dumbo Ears. (This is really the last time I am going to mention my ears!)

Georgie has reddish-brown hair, greenish-brown eyes, braces, and really cool glasses with bright red rims. He is already eleven and is almost twice my size. He is good at games where being big is an advantage, like basketball and  football. My best sports are soccer and baseball because I am wicked fast and very excellent at catching flies.

 I have brown hair, brown eyes, and a whitish scar on my thumb where a fishhook stabbed me when I was on a lake with my dad. I was eight and fooling around. Don't ask.

Georgie and I go to the same school, have always had the same teacher, and in the summer, always go to camp in Maine.

"I was down here looking for black widow spiders," Georgie continued. "I figured if I caught one in a jar, we could use it to scare your sister. But this"—Georgie brought his arm around and held up a yellowed envelope with one corner ripped off—"was completely hidden between those two boards." He pointed under the stairs, but I took my eyes off the envelope for only a second. "It's addressed to my house, but the name is"—he squinted at the envelope— "G. J. Prott."

"Probably there was somebody named G. J. Prott who lived here before you guys," I said.

Georgie nodded. "Look what was in the envelope!"

He held out a piece of paper folded up small, then opened it. Inside were a silvery metal heart on a silvery metal chain and one penny.

"A penny? Not exactly treasure, Georgie."

"Yeah, but this necklace is probably real silver. And what if there's more hidden stuff? Like gold and diamonds."

I picked up the necklace and held it high between us. The lightbulb on the basement rafters was not very bright, but the heart sparkled as it spun slowly.

"I bet a hypnotist could use this to hypnotize people," I said.

Georgie didn't say anything. Maybe I'd sort of hypnotized him.

I placed the heart necklace back on the paper in Georgie's hand and examined the coin. The back looked a lot different from any other penny I'd ever seen, but the front had the same face on it: Abraham Lincoln, our sixteenth president.

(Glenn Philips, the smartest kid in my class, can name all the presidents *and* all the vice presidents. In order!)

I looked at the date on the coin. "This penny was made in 1909."

That snapped Georgie out of his trance. He grabbed the penny and peered at it closely. "That means it's over a hundred years old."

One of us said, "Whoa."

I don't remember who.

Georgie set the penny down on the paper next to the heart necklace and handed it all to me. He held the envelope up so that we both could look at it.

The postmark—that's the inky stuff in the circle

Really old!

that tells when and where the letter was mailed—was kind of smeary. We could read "Calif." and "Mar 11 9:43 AM 195," but the last number of the year and whatever city in California were unreadable. The stamp was blue-green, with *Wildlife Conservation* across the top, *3¢ United States Postage 3¢* on the bottom, and in the middle, a big fish jumping from a stream next to the tiny words *King Salmon*.

"I've got it!" Georgie said suddenly. "Someone didn't want anyone to know where this letter came from, so they ripped off the corner where the return address was and smeared up the postmark on purpose." He pointed at the unfolded paper in my hand. "And there's something real suspicious about putting plain white paper in an envelope."

I shrugged. "Maybe whoever sent it just wanted to keep the stuff inside from flopping around. And maybe the envelope got ripped and smudged by accident."

"Nah," Georgie said. "We are on to something big. That coin. It's probably worth millions."

I didn't think it could be worth that much, but I

looked at it closely. "I don't think I've held anything that was over a hundred years old before."

"Maybe this," Georgie said, jabbing at the paper in my hand, "has invisible ink on it."

I held it up to the light. "It looks like plain, ordinary paper to me."

"Look, if it had a secret map on it, you wouldn't be able to see it. And maybe, since you can't see it, that proves it's there." Even though we were alone, Georgie lowered his voice like he didn't want anyone else to hear. "If we could read it, we'd know where the rest of the treasure is buried." He touched the postmark. "Probably in California."

I took the envelope from Georgie and pointed at the stamp. "Probably in the bottom of a stream with a bunch of king salmon jumping all around," I teased.

Georgie tried to get me into a headlock, but I squirgled out of his grip and jumped away. (There is actually no such word as "squirgled," but since what I actually did was to squirm and wiggle . . . Well, you get it.)

"I don't know about any buried treasure," I said,

"but let's get on your computer and see what we can find about this old penny."

We trotted upstairs to his bedroom and turned on his computer. While it booted up, Georgie dug around in his closet for an old magician's set that he said had a potion that would make invisible ink turn visible.

I did a web search for "United States coins" and found a site that listed every United States coin ever made. Did you know that we used to have three-cent coins?

Then I searched for "Lincoln penny value" and discovered that it's a Lincoln *cent*, not *penny*. The word "cent" means that there are one hundred of them in every dollar and is almost the same as the word "century" (one hundred years, duh!). I don't know where the word "penny" comes from—and neither does anyone else. I looked it up. But there are pennies in England, and I'm guessing that there are one hundred of them to the pound or euro or whatever the people in England use for money. I wonder if every country uses money that breaks into one hundred smaller pieces. If you know of a country that doesn't, please go to my website. I'm making a list.

Georgie had opened his magic set and was struggling to unscrew the potion bottle when I saw that there was a little letter *S* under the 1909 next to Abraham Lincoln's chest.

Georgie grunted as he got the top off the potion bottle. "Rats, it's all dried up."

"Hey, Georgie," I said after reading more of the web page. "It says here that this little *S* means that this penny was made in San Francisco."

Made in San Francisco— another clue!

Georgie leaned over, took a quick look at the coin, and nodded a couple of times. "California. See? I told you so." He put on his magician's hat and bow tie and began waving his wand around, trying to make some fake flowers appear and disappear.

I clicked around the Internet until I found a site that

 showed how much old Lincoln cents were worth.

Georgie tapped me on the shoulder. He held the coin up, then closed his left hand around it, waved his right hand over his left, wiggled his fingers, twisted his wrists around each other, opened his hands . . . and abracadabra, the coin was gone. An instant later (I could not tell how he did it), the coin was back . . . this time in his right hand! He was actually really good.

"You never showed me that trick before. How do you do it?" I asked.

Georgie shook his head. "The Great Georgio never reveals his secrets." He held the old penny between two fingers. "So, how much is this worth?"

I looked back at the screen and read aloud: "'Value depends upon the condition of the coin.' I think that means how new it looks."

Georgie examined the coin closely. "It looks pretty new to me." Then The Great Georgio did his sleight of hand again. This time I watched super carefully, but I still couldn't figure it out. I turned back to the screen and found the listing for a 1909 Lincoln cent, but I was still thinking hard about the trick. I should have been paying more attention to the computer screen.

"Only three dollars," I said.

"Huh?! Come on. Is that all?"

"That's what it says. Three bucks."

"Darn," Georgie said.

I thought the coin was worth three dollars.

I was wrong.

And the mistake was my fault. I completely admit it in writing *right now* and *right here*. Georgie's magic sort of distracted me, so I looked at the wrong line in the list of coin values. The 1909 Lincoln cent with *no* mint mark (which means it was made in Philadelphia) was the coin that was worth three dollars. The coin with the *S* (San Francisco) was worth a lot more . . . but I didn't know that until much later. And my mistake made our lives a whole lot more complicated. You'll see how if you read on.

Georgie set the coin down next to the computer keyboard and started putting his magician stuff back into its box. I picked up the torn envelope. "This stamp is really old. Maybe it's worth something," I said.

"Yeah, maybe," Georgie muttered.

I switched my search from coin collecting, which on the web page is called numismatics (*new-miz-MAT-iks*), to stamp collecting, which is called philately (*fih-LAT-eh-lee*). Those are two excellent words that I am going to memorize so that I can use them in a conversation with my dad, who I am sure knows them because he reads everything and has a great vocabulary and knows all kinds of weird things that no one else does.

You can probably tell by now that I like words. Maybe that's why I like writing. I will definitely put some superlative (*soo-PER-lah-tiv*)—which means better than excellent—words into this book.

I heard a match strike. Georgie had lit a stubby candle from his magic set and was holding the unfolded paper above it. I looked at him with a question wrinkling up my forehead.

"Heat the paper, and the secret writing will appear," he explained.

He held the paper over the flame. Secret writing did

not appear, but he did set fire to one corner. He blew it out, pinched the candle flame between his fingers (Georgie is tough!), and plopped down on his bed while I read about old postage stamps on the Internet.

A few moments later, we heard his father call, "Georgie! I smell something burning. What's going on?"

"Just a candle, Dad. We're trying to do some magic."

"Be careful, huh? And come here when you're done."

I like Georgie's father. He's way older than my dad, but he cooks really excellent pancakes. I don't re-member Georgie's mother. She died when we were two years old.

I went to another web page and there, along with lots of other old stamps, was the three-cent jumping king salmon.

"I found the stamp."

Georgie stood up and peered over my shoulder.

"The stamp was first made in 1956," I continued. "And look. It says here that the cost of mailing a letter increased to four cents on August 1, 1958, so this envelope"—I pointed at "3¢" on the stamp—"had to be mailed before then. Sheesh, it costs way more to mail a letter now."

(I wonder what it will cost to mail a letter fifty years from now. You can take a guess by going to my website: CheesieMack.com. Maybe when I get enough guesses, I'll put them into some kind of Internet time capsule, and fifty years in the future I'll open it and see how close we were.)

Georgie pointed at the picture of the stamp on the computer screen. "Are there king salmon in California?"

I shrugged. I'd seen a TV show once about salmon swimming upstream to lay eggs, but I couldn't remember what state it was in.

"Is it worth anything?" Georgie asked.

"Can't tell. This is all about stamps in what they call *mint condition*." We looked at the wavy lines of black ink crossing our stamp. "This one's *canceled*. I don't think it's worth anything. Not even three cents."

(I'm collecting images of cool stamps from around the world. If you have a favorite, please send it to me along with a clever, weird, or funny caption to go with it. There are examples on my website.)

Suddenly Georgie grabbed a pencil from his desk,

held it sideways, and started to smudge the lead across the partly burnt paper.

"Why're you scribbling on it?"

"To see if someone left dents when they wrote on the piece of paper that used to be on top of this piece of paper," he said, head down and concentrating. "I saw this in a movie once. It was about a murder and the killer's name . . ."

In the corner farthest away from the scorch marks, a single word began to take shape. We both stared at it.

"I can't read it," Georgie mumbled.

"I think," I whispered, "it says 'EUREKA.'"

I couldn't help whispering. If you're doing something like making invisible old words reappear, you just automatically get quiet. I could tell from Georgie's expression that he didn't know the word *EUREKA*.

"It means," I said, "something like 'hooray' or 'yippee.' My dad says you yell it when you find something."

"Like treasure," he said very softly.

Someone said "Whoa" again, and I'm pretty sure it was me.

Chapter 3
Really Bad News

We sat for a while thinking about what to do next, but since neither of us had an idea, we decided to get our mitts, go to the park, and hit some flies before it got too dark.

When we got downstairs, Mr. Sinkoff, who was sitting at the kitchen table with a bunch of papers spread out, stopped us by holding up his hand.

"Georgie," he said seriously, "I'm afraid I've got some bad news."

Georgie and I stood looking at his father for what seemed like a really long and awkward time, but it couldn't have been more than a few seconds.

I mean, here you are reading this book, and you want to know what the bad news was, but there's this long sentence that you're reading right now that actually doesn't take all that long to read, but because you're in a hurry to learn about the bad news, this sentence seems to take a lot longer. Kind of like that.

Mr. Sinkoff cleared his throat, but the *scraff-scraff* sound he made must have done more clogging than clearing because he had to cough twice before he finally looked at me and suggested it might be time for me to go home. Georgie's eyebrows were waggling up and down the way they do when he gets nervous.

I walked to the back door very slowly, sort of leaning with my head tilted, aiming my ear, straining to hear what was happening.

I'm usually not super nosy, but Georgie is my best friend, and I was thinking that it must be really serious because Mr. Sinkoff was almost whispering. I had my hand on the back doorknob when Georgie screamed, "OH, NO!"

Then silence again. Bad silence.

As I stepped outside into the twilight, I could hear everything everywhere: crickets . . . my dog,

Deeb, barking . . . the *brrr-rum* of a motorcycle a couple of streets away . . . some girls singing jump-rope rhymes . . . and a faraway plane. But everything in my mind was flat. I wasn't thinking about anything. I just stood there. Deeb stopped barking.

Then Georgie came running out the back door, yelling or crying or both, "This really stinks!"

He ran right past me. And then he was out of sight, racing out the won't-close-gate into the gully.

I ran after him.

Then I stopped.

Then I ran again.

Then I just walked. I knew where he was going. If he was crying, he'd want time to stop before I got there. Georgie has three brothers, but they are grown-up and don't live with him, so he is sort of an only child, and he's not used to crying in front of anyone.

So I walked.

I've noticed a funny thing about crying. Little kids actually seem to like doing it. When you're small, you wail and wail. It's loud. You make enough noise to block out the rest of the world. And the crying all by itself fills you up so much that you forget why you started in the first place and just sort of hide in your own noise. But when you get to almost eleven, like me, mostly you don't do that anymore.

I walked exactly 119 steps downstream from the path between our two houses (98 steps if Georgie's counting . . . his steps are bigger). That's where the creek, which almost never has any water in it, goes under a road. Just above the creek bed, there's a four-foot-wide metal pipe that goes through the concrete

wall that holds up the road. Once inside the pipe, we're completely out of sight of everyone, and there's a sort of echo that makes everything we say sound more important, so Georgie and I have turned it into our secret clubhouse. We don't have a club or anything. No members. No secret passwords. But we couldn't think of a better name.

That's where I knew I would find him. And I did.

When Georgie looked up, I saw that his eyes had that fat, swelled-up look that kids get when they've been crying. He sniffed, then rubbed his nose hard.

"I've got some really bad news . . . . Cheesie."

Please look at the previous sentence.

I put those sixteen dots between the last two words because even though Georgie was talking at regular speed, my mind was zooming so fast that the split second between "bad news" and "Cheesie" lasted for a long time.

Here's what the noise of my thinking sounded like:

1. Georgie was really mad. But he didn't sound

a bit sad or afraid. I think dying would make him sad and afraid. So I figured he didn't have cancer or Ebola or stuff.

2. Maybe we weren't friends anymore. But why would his father say he had bad news? It didn't make sense.

3. That left just one possibility: I was pretty sure Georgie was moving away.

Georgie sniffed again, loud, and then said a word six times in a row that the people who print these books told me I definitely could not write. Then he took a deep breath and said, "Cheesie, my father told me I can't go to camp."

I hadn't thought of *that*. We loved camp, and this year would be our fifth summer in a row. It lasts six weeks and is maximum fun.

"My father said he can't afford it. He got laid off." Georgie's face was all scrunched, and his eyes started to get even puffier and redder.

Georgie's father ~~works~~ worked for some kind of technology company. He's a microwave transmission engineer. I don't know what that means, but I know it does not have anything to do with the microwave I use to heat frozen burritos.

Georgie picked up some pebbles. I leaned backward because I thought he was going to fling them hard. But he just clinked them against the metal wall of our clubhouse and slumped his head. I had never seen him this miserable.

Then I felt miserable because this summer at camp was going to be our best yet. It has to do with Big Guys and Little Guys.

Granpa (I forgot to mention that he's the camp director) and his staff of counselors divide the boys at Camp Windward into two groups. Big Guys stay up later, play some different sports like lacrosse and flag football, and have dances and stuff with Camp Leeward, the girls' camp next door.

Georgie and I have been Little Guys for the last four years. This year we would still be Little Guys, but our cabin would be the *oldest* of the Little Guys, which is terrific. We'd get to be in charge of Little Guys campfires, movie nights, the skit and talent show, color war, and lots of other great stuff. Next year we'll be the youngest of the Big Guys. Not so good.

Granpa's ex-wife owns both the boys' camp and the girls' camp. She is not my grandmother because she married Granpa fifteen years after my father was born, and they got divorced long before I was born. Everyone at camp calls her Aunt Lois, and so do I.

"This ruins the whole summer," Georgie muttered softly, and then we sat in our clubhouse without talking. Finally I said something I didn't really even think about before I said it.

"If you can't go to camp, then I won't go, either."

After I said it, I wasn't sure I really meant it.

Georgie lifted his head slowly and stared at me for a long time.

"You serious?"

Was I? Summer camp in Maine was my most favorite thing I did all year.

I looked at my best friend. He looked awful.

I felt terrible.

I swallowed hard, then gave a big nod. I knew I had made the right decision.

Chapter 4
The Mouse Plot

My decision not to go to camp was huge news in my house that night. Here's what Mom, Dad, Granpa, Goon, and Deeb said:

1. "Ha-ha."
2. "No way you two are staying home alone. Unless Georgie has adult supervision, you'll go down to the limo garage every day."
3. Said nothing. Tried to make me laugh with a squinty-evil-eye, but I didn't even smile.
4. "Woof."
5. "We're going to have a lot of fun without you."

(I mixed them up. Can you guess who said what? The answers are on page 42.)

Then I got an idea. Sometimes I get an idea that I

know is terrible, but I have to say it out loud because even though I think I know the idea is terrible, maybe I'm wrong, and it's a good idea.

"Granpa? Maybe you could let Georgie go to camp for free. You know, like getting a scholarship."

Remember I mentioned how Granpa likes to argue and get mad? Well, I shouldn't have been surprised by his reaction.

"That's a dumb idea. That's a dumb idea six different ways!" He was talking loudly. "Dumb Idea Number First." He held up one finger and waved it around. "I don't know a blue-blessed thing about how Lois runs her camps. Money-wise, I mean. Scholarship? Forget it. She doesn't tell me anything. I'm just a hired gun."

"Dumb Idea Number Second." He stuck up two fingers in a V and jerked them around so fast that I leaned backward a little bit to get out of the way. "I happen to know that Lois is almost broke, very cash-short, out of money. Dumb Idea Number Third—"

"Hey, Pop," Dad interrupted. "Your Dumb Idea

Number First totally contradicts your Dumb Idea Number Second. How can you not know a blue-blessed anything and also know that she's out of money?"

Granpa ignored the interruption.

"Dumb Idea Number Third. If Georgie doesn't pay, camp won't mean as much to him, and he'll just goof off all summer."

"But I get in free because you're the director," I said, "and I don't goof off all summer."

Granpa ignored me, too. "Dumb Idea Number Fourth . . ." There was a pause while Granpa waved both hands excitedly. Finally he said, "I can't remember. And Fifth and Sixth, I found out this week that I've got two empty slots on the camp staff that'll cost Lois extra money to fill. The camp nurse just got a job on a cruise ship, and your counselor from last year has decided to bicycle across Canada."

Granpa stared at me like it was my fault.

I have to admit I was having trouble concentrating on what Granpa was saying because he was holding up only five fingers, but he was already up to Dumb Idea Number Sixth. And I was also thinking about

Scott Dutcher, my last summer's counselor. He was the bicycle-across-Canada guy. Dutcher was this awesome athlete who could do eleven one-armed push-ups, tell very scary lights-out stories, and eat an entire, full-size hot dog, with mustard and relish and tons of goop dripping off of it, in one bite.

*Do not attempt until you can do eleven one-armed push-ups.

At camp we called that "doing a Dutcher." Me and all the other campers really liked him. Normally I would have been upset that my favorite counselor wasn't coming back, but since I wasn't going to camp unless Georgie got a scholarship, and Granpa had pretty much said that Georgie wasn't getting a scholarship, it didn't matter.

Plus my mother had just served a late dessert: rice pudding, my favorite.

I really like rice pudding with raisins, which is the way my dad makes it, but he doesn't cook very often. My sister hates raisins, so Mom makes it without them and gives me a bunch on the side to stick in. But it's not the same. When you cook raisins inside rice pudding, they get all plumpy. Otherwise, they're sort of dried and hard. I was poking them into my pudding when Goon interrupted.

"What're those? Dried roach brains?"

Granpa jumped in. "You want to know about roaches? Let me tell you about the bugs underneath Fenway Park. I'm talking cockroaches the size of trombones! I was seventeen, selling ice cream at the ballpark, and—"

Just then the back door opened, and conversation stopped.

Everyone (even Deeb, who looked up, yipped softly, and put her head back down) knew it was Georgie because no one else comes in the back way.

I totally expected him to still be upset about not going to camp, but he was grinning, bouncing from foot to foot, and carrying a paper bag. I waited for him to speak, but he just gave me eye signals to come with him somewhere else. I picked up my rice pudding, yelled "Doin' a Dutcher!" and slid the whole thing into my mouth.

Goon yelled, "Slob!"

My mom shook her head.

Georgie and I ran upstairs to my room. Deeb bounded after us.

"I have the greatest plan," Georgie announced.

I was trying to pay attention, but I was having trouble swallowing.

He opened the bag. It was filled with white mice! I coughed, almost choked, and spewed a few globbets. Deeb, who had been sniffing at the bag, immediately licked them up.

(The rice pudding that I spewed really looked like whatever globbets would be if *globbets* was really a word, so I convinced the people who publish this book to leave it in. But I made globbets up, so don't use it in school writing. Your teacher won't understand.)

"After you went home, I went downtown with

my dad." Georgie was talking fast. "And while he was in the hardware store, I went into Corvi's pet shop. You know, across from the library, just to look around. They sell mice for snakes to eat. Today they had way-too-way many, so Mrs. Corvi gave me these for free."

There must have been a dozen in the bag. But I didn't have a clue what this had to do with anything, and to be honest, I was surprised that Georgie, who had been so miserable about not going to camp, was now so excited. I must have looked confused. And anyway, my cheeks were all puffed out with pudding.

"You don't have a snake," I plorfed through my pudding, then swallowed. (I'm having fun making up words!)

Georgie began knocking his knuckles on my skull. "Hello? We take the bag to school. Let them go during graduation. Screaming. Yelling. Get it?"

There was a one-second pause of dead silence, then the two of us were screaming and yelling. We stopped suddenly when we saw Goon standing in my doorway. She was smiling.

"What?" I asked.

"Nothing," she said sweetly, and walked away.

"Do you think she heard us?" I asked.

"Who cares?" Georgie replied. "This is the best idea I have ever had."

The next morning Georgie, holding his bag of mice, walked in my back door almost an hour early. I was finishing breakfast, already dressed and ready. Mom never even had to remind me. I was that excited. And not about graduation.

My mom is very intelligent. I should not have gotten ready so early. She suspected something. So when Georgie wanted to whisper about the mice, I gave him a shut-up look, glanced over my shoulder at Mom, and changed the subject as we headed up to my room.

"I looked in the phone book for someone named Prott," I said.

"Yeah, that's good," Georgie replied, staring into his bag of mice. I could tell he had forgotten not only about camp but also all about the heart necklace, the 1909 coin, and the hidden *Eureka* word we'd found.

"There's a G. J. Prott who lives right here in Gloucester," I said.

"But the letter came from California."

I picked the phone book up off my desk and opened it to the Ps.

I pointed to a name: "Prott G J 207 Eureka Av Glou."

"So?"

"So? Eureka!" I almost shouted. "Eureka! It's the hidden word. This has to be the right Prott. The heart necklace? The coin? Remember?" I let that sink in while I scribbled the address on a page I tore from the phone book. It was the page that went from "Tobacco" to "Toilet Seats." Since nobody smokes in my house, and we already have a seat on every toilet, I was pretty sure that no one would ever notice that it was missing.

I stuffed the T–T page into my jacket pocket. "Where's Eureka Avenue?"

Georgie shrugged an I-don't-know, held up the bag of mice, and whispered, "Come on. We can find that stuff out later. Right now we've got to do our most excellent plan." Then he grinned the most evil grin I have ever seen.

We hustled downstairs.

"What's in the bag?" Goon demanded when we got to the back door. Middle school was already out for the summer, and she was mad that she had to go to my graduation.

We ignored her. She was talking to Alex Welch's brother, Kevin. He's in Goon's grade. She thinks he is her boyfriend. He goes to our camp every summer and is really good at sports. After one of Goon's soccer games, she dared Kevin to prove that he was strong enough to toss me into the Dumpster behind the gym. You can probably guess the rest. I could write a book about why I don't like him. But don't worry, I'm not going to. Alex Welch is our suspect for the bike seat dog-pooper. He's a dork.

"Georgie and I are going to ride to school!" I yelled to Mom. "We'll meet you there!"

"Feed your dog first!" she shouted back. "And stay clean for graduation!"

My dog is a springer spaniel with big, floppy ears.

We got her when I was three. Her actual name is Pandora, but because mythology says that some lady named Pandora let demons out of a box that she wasn't supposed to open, I gave my Pandora the nick-name Devil, which somehow got changed to Deeble, then Deebie, and that's how we ended up with Deeb. She is a terrific dog, except that she really smells like a dog. I don't mind it much, but visitors sometimes complain.

Deeb was waiting on the back porch, where we keep a plastic barrel of kibble. I could tell she was hungry because she was jumping all four feet off the ground over and over. I poured some food in her dish, knelt down, and pretended to eat it. She stopped jumping.

"You are gross," Georgie said. "And so is your dog." He was holding his nose.

I ignored him. When Deeb tried to come close, I growled at her and showed her my teeth until she backed away. Then I "ate" some more, making lots of chewing, slurping, grunting sounds. When I was finished, I stood up and looked at Deeb. She looked

at me, then the dish of food, then back at me. I waited a couple of seconds, then nodded and made a small grunt. Deeb ran to the dish and chowed down.

This is not exactly a book on dog training, but I know something that is really important if you're a kid with a dog.

In the wild, dogs live in packs, so they naturally expect to run around with lots of other dogs. It's in their genes, I guess. Most pet dogs, however, live with only humans for company. So, even though humans sometimes think their dogs act almost human, IMO it's actually the dogs that think their humans are some kind of giant dog. There has to be a leader of every dog pack. It's called the Alpha Dog. I read about it on the Internet. So you should want the leader of the pack in your house to be a human . . . unless you want your dog to be the boss of your whole family.

In the woods or the jungle, the Alpha Dog always eats first. So I make certain Deeb knows that I am the Alpha Dog in the best way that her dog brain can understand. I pretend to eat the food until I'm "full." Then it's her turn.

You should try it. It really works. I've got a great dog.

Kevin's father drove up. Alex leaned out the window, stuck his thumbs in his ears, and waggled his fingers. We ignored him. Goon and Kevin walked by us on their way to the car.

"What's in the bag?" Goon asked again. She didn't even wait for me not to reply.

I brushed kibble dust off my good pants. Georgie wrapped the top of his bag of mice around a handlebar grip. And we took off toward school. The Mouse Plot was under way!

CHAPTER 4α
Chee and the Taug

Capt. Chee Seemak licked his lips, brushed the worm powder off his uniform, then stood and pushed the dish away. He stared at the Taug, then nodded. The beast, a thick smell oozing from its oily fur, unrolled its long black-and-orange tongue and licked up the scraps.

Sinko Jorsh came lumbering into the chamber, took one look, and muttered in disgust, "Grarq."

"A man has to eat something," Chee said. "It's crazy to pass up nutrition, no matter what it is."

The worldwide famine had made real food almost nonexistent.

Jorsh moved his metallic mouth into something that was almost a smile and held up a transparent

54

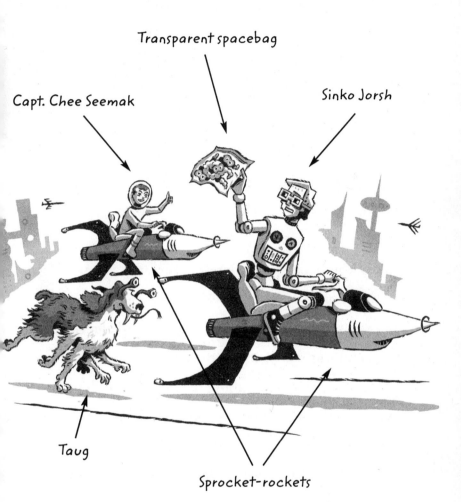

Transparent spacebag

Capt. Chee Seemak

Sinko Jorsh

Taug

Sprocket-rockets

spacebag. In it was a scurrying mass of small creatures. The Taug, by nature an intensely curious beast, flicked its tri-forked tongue toward the spacebag, but Jorsh lifted it out of reach.

Chee's eyes widened. "Great work, Jorsh! You may have found the answer to the food crisis. Let's get those mini-clones to the university."

Moments later they were astride their sprocket-rockets heading for the Enlargement Lab.

* * *

Okay, this book is not science fiction. But just now I got to thinking how I would write this whole narrative— my dad says that's what you call a story if someone like me is telling it—if it really was science fiction. So I wrote the paragraphs above to show you. Of course, it would still be about me, but I wouldn't be called Cheesie. It's a great name for a kid, but not for a space hero. (Actually, I might decide to call myself Chee when I get to high school.)

And in the science fiction version of my story, Georgie Sinkoff (Sinko Jorsh) would be a half-human and half-robotic giant or something else strong. And

I'd have Jorsh's dad building death-ray lasers instead of microwave stuff.

The Taug (Deeb) would have six legs. Maybe more.

Granpa would run a training camp for space warriors. My dad would own and pilot a small fleet of passenger spaceships. And my mom would still be an air-traffic controller, except now she'd work at the Glah Star Spaceport instead of Logan Airport.

Goon would be a hideously deformed mutant.

Because it's science fiction, I call this Chapter 4α. That's not an A, by the way. It's an alpha, the first letter of the Greek alphabet. I guess that's why we have an ALPHA-bet. Duh. Mom said that Greek letters are used all the time in science, so I figured they'd be good for science fiction, too.

Maybe my next book will be sci-fi.

Chapter 5
The Haunted Toad
and the Runaway Rodents

Georgie and I have been riding our bikes to school for about two years. Before that, our parents said we were too young, even though we are both very excellent bike riders.

Although Gloucester is right on the ocean, it is very hilly—something to do with immense glaciers that pushed huge rocks thousands and thousands of years ago and left them right here. About halfway to school we bike by The Haunted Toad. Then we twist and turn downhill for several blocks past a bunch of stores and stuff until we get to the street our school is on.

The Haunted Toad is a big, old, dark green-gray house with a nose-high fence—my nose, not Georgie's—

that goes all around the front yard. We didn't always
call it The Haunted Toad. At first we just called it The
Toad because its outside looked dry and warty, and
Georgie and I thought it looked like a huge, squatting
amphibian, which is what toads and frogs are.

Toad, frog . . . what's the difference?

1. Toads have dry, warty skin. Frogs have
   smooth, wet skin. (Frogs are not slimy.
   I have held them. I know.)

2. Toads are toothless. Frogs have little teeth. (Their teeth are really tiny. I have touched them and have never been bitten.)

3. Toads have shorter hind legs than frogs. (I do not have personal knowledge of this. I read about it. But if I ever get a toad and a frog together, I will measure and put the results on my website.)

4. Toads lay eggs hooked together in long strings. Frogs lay one egg at a time in clumps on the surface of the water. (I have seen clumps of frog eggs in the creek between my house and Georgie's. Lots of times.)

5. Toads have poison sacs behind their eyes. Frogs are harmless. (Deeb bit a toad once and spit it out immediately!)

And you *cannot* get warts by touching either a frog or a toad. I have held frogs lots of times and a toad once, and I have zero warts. It's a myth.

Even though we passed The Toad twice every school day, going and coming home, neither Georgie nor I had ever, never seen any sign of life. No lights. No mailman. No gardener. Not even that bluish glow that comes from a television set. So we decided it was deserted. But we didn't exactly think there was anything weird about it . . . not yet.

Then one day about a year ago, maybe near the end of fourth grade, we were biking home from school when I suddenly jammed on my brakes just as we were passing by The Toad. I stopped so fast that Georgie almost crashed into me. I was staring up at the old house . . . and I wasn't saying anything.

"What?" Georgie asked me.

I just stared. I didn't even turn my head to look at him.

"What?" he repeated in a softer, more nervous voice.

"Something moved," I whispered. "I saw something move behind that curtain upstairs."

"Which one?" Georgie whispered, looking up at The Toad, his eyebrows waggling.

I pointed up at a window, and Georgie followed my

finger with his eyes. We stared for a long time. Then he looked at me, and I looked at him, and he said very seriously, "I saw it, too."

Of course Georgie hadn't seen anything. And neither had I. He just said that to go along with me. I think here's why we did it. Sometimes kids like to make up scary things just to scare themselves. So from then on, Georgie and I would pretend to see shapes moving inside the old house whenever we rode our bikes past. And that's when it became The Haunted Toad.

So this day, the day of our fifth-grade graduation, with the two of us dressed up, we rode past The Haunted Toad, and Georgie as usual pointed at a third-floor window and pretended to be terrified.

I started to let out one of my super-scary soft-and-spooky howls. (It's kind of an "ow-hooo-eeeee." I do it very well. At night sometimes when my parents are downstairs, I howl it, and even though it doesn't really scare my sister, she gets mad at me anyway.)

But I was only starting into the "hooo" part when something I had seen a million times stopped the sound half out of my throat.

I braked my bike and stared. I was fumbling in my jacket pocket when Georgie asked, "What?" He looked at me and then back up at The Haunted Toad. Then back at me. Then back and forth one more time.

"What?"

I couldn't say anything. I bet I looked like I had seen a ghost!

I pointed at the street sign we had passed to and from school every day since kindergarten. Then I pointed at the number on the mailbox in front of The Haunted Toad. Then I pointed at the address I had written on the yellow phone-book page in my hand: 207 Eureka Avenue.

G. J. Prott lived in The Haunted Toad!

Just then one of the mice in the paper bag decided the time was right for an escape. It—he or she . . . mice probably know the difference, but I can't tell— bit a hole through the bag and stuck its nose out. Georgie instantly folded the bag to cover the hole and rode off toward school.

"Come on!" he yelled.

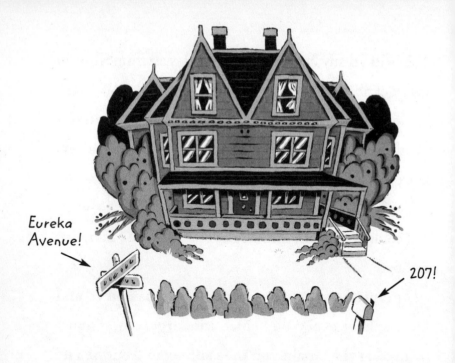

Eureka Avenue!

207!

I took one last look at the address I'd written, then biked after him at full speed.

Lots of kids were already inside the auditorium when we walked in. Georgie's bag now had two bite holes in it, one of which had a mouse head poking out. He tucked it tightly under his jacket.

"I don't know, Cheesie. Maybe this isn't such a good—"

I raised my hand to stop him from finishing. Only four rows away, my sister and Kevin Welch were talking to his brother, Alex. She pointed at us, and Alex hurried over.

"My brother and your sister want to know what's in the bag," he said. Alex looked like he didn't know what he was talking about, which is pretty usual for him.

"What bag?" Georgie asked.

"Yeah, what bag?" I echoed.

"I don't know." Alex shrugged. "They just told me to say that."

Georgie suddenly jerked, said something that sounded like "Eee-yeen!" and pulled me toward a side door, leaving Alex standing there looking stupid, which is pretty usual for him.

In the empty corridor outside the auditorium, Georgie began squirming like crazy. "Help me, Cheesie! One of the mice just went into my shirt!"

Six Georgie twitches, five Georgie hops, and four Georgie contortions later, I pulled his shirt out of the back of his pants and a mouse dropped to the floor. It skittered under a wall of lockers.

"No way, Cheesie! This isn't going to work."

Clutching the bag tightly with both hands, he ran down the corridor to his locker and yanked it open. Luckily Georgie never uses his locker for anything except storing his lunch, so there was no lock on it and he didn't have to waste time with a combination. The bag was totally coming apart, and he was losing mice fast.

One dropped to the floor. I grabbed it. Another crawled out and scampered up Georgie's arm onto his shoulder. I grabbed that one, too. Georgie shoved the bag of mice into his locker and slammed the door shut.

I didn't even have time to ask what the heck I was supposed to do with a mouse in each hand when the door to the auditorium flew open. Goon was holding it and grinning big-time as Mrs. Crespo came striding through, heading right toward Georgie and me.

Chapter 6
Partially Expelled

Mrs. Crespo, our principal, has been at our school for 247 years. I'm exaggerating, of course, but I know it's a really big number. She was actually my dad's fourth-grade teacher, and he told me she was the youngest, shortest, funniest, and strictest teacher he ever had. Here's what I know about Mrs. Crespo and those four things:

1. She's not young anymore. She must be way more than forty or sixty or something.
2. She is very short, almost as short as I am.
3. She grins a lot, which I think is unusual for school principals.
4. She is very strict, which I think is usual for school principals, because principals have

to punish the kids who do bad stuff like
bring mice to school.

As Mrs. Crespo approached, I stuck both my hands,
a mouse in each, into my pants pockets. She passed
Georgie, who was leaning against his locker and
making *plip-plop* noises with his lips so Mrs. Crespo
wouldn't hear the mice scratching around inside. She
stopped about five inches in front of me.

"Your sister says you have a bag I should look into.
May I see it, please?"

It was one of those moments when a kid's stomach
gets all hot and watery because you know you're probably in big trouble. Even so, I thought of three things
I could do:

1. I could say "What bag?" like I did with
   Alex, but Mrs. Crespo's a million times
   smarter than Alex.

2. If I had another bag—an empty bag—
   I could show that to her. It wouldn't
   exactly be a lie because Mrs. Crespo didn't
   exactly ask for a bag of mice. And I kind of
   remembered that there might be an empty

lunch bag in my locker, which was in the next hallway. But I wasn't sure.

3. I could say I didn't have any bag. It wouldn't exactly be a lie because Mrs. Crespo asked for *my* bag, and the bag of mice that by this time was probably in shreds inside Georgie's locker was *Georgie's* bag, and actually I had never even touched it . . . only looked inside it.

But before I could say anything, Georgie abruptly yanked open his locker and pointed. There was a very

Big trouble!

short no-one-made-a-sound, and then Mrs. Crespo's mouth jumped into a big circle and a loud "oooh" came out.

One second later my principal's arm whizzed by me and slammed the locker shut.

Mrs. Crespo's circle mouth turned into a line. She looked really strict. She had a you-better-explain look on her face. Georgie and I were going to have to tell the truth. And when we did, bad things would happen. Mrs. Crespo would tell my mother, who is a little bit afraid of mice and crawlies. Mom would think we did a really bad thing, and I'd be punished. Probably no TV or computer games for the rest of my life.

Georgie looked down at his feet and said, "I did it. Those are my mice. Cheesie didn't do anything."

"Go on," Mrs. Crespo said. Goon was now standing right behind Mrs. Crespo.

Georgie mumbled, "I got them at the pet sto—"

Mrs. Crespo waited for him to continue, but he couldn't talk. His eyebrows were waggling, but his voice was paralyzed. He looked at me helplessly, and even though Goon was grinning wickedly, I ignored her and started talking. I told Mrs. Crespo what Georgie had originally planned to do at graduation: cross his eyes, hold his breath, pretend to barf—the whole list is way earlier in this book, in Chapter 1.

"But he wasn't going to do any of those things anymore. None of them. He was only just bringing mice to school." As soon as I said it, I realized how lame it sounded.

Mrs. Crespo turned away from me and faced Georgie. "Is this true?"

Georgie nodded.

It was exactly then that I, both hands still in my pockets, suddenly twitched my left arm and half spun around. This surprised Mrs. Crespo, who turned toward me, waiting for an explanation. I said nothing. I wasn't about to explain that the mouse in my left hand had almost wriggled free.

Mrs. Crespo stared back and forth from me to Georgie and then began to tap her fingers together. I had seen her do this lots of times before. It meant that she had already decided that someone was guilty and was now trying to think up the right punishment. We were doomed.

"Well then, George Harrison Sinkoff, you will stay right by my side until graduation starts, at which time you will take your seat and behave yourself. If you do not, you will be PARTIALLY EXPELLED from school for the rest of the year. And since the rest of the school year consists of just one event, your fifth-grade class party, being PARTIALLY EXPELLED will consist of coming to the party and sitting by yourself doing absolutely nothing while everyone else has fun. Is that clear?"

Georgie's eyebrows stopped waggling for a moment, and he nodded.

"And you, Mr. Mack . . . As accomplice to this mischief, you will stay with me and Mr. Sinkoff at all times and make certain that he does exactly as I said. And if he misbehaves, you, Mr. Mack, will also be PARTIALLY EXPELLED."

I nodded seriously and asked, "May I go to the bathroom?"

Mrs. Crespo nodded. "You have two minutes."

Hands still in my pockets, I walked to the end of the hall and turned into the corridor where the Boys room is. Once out of their sight, I sprinted, arms flying, a mouse in each hand. I shot right past the bathroom and was out the side door in less than ten seconds. I ran to the grassy field and carefully placed the two mice on the ground. "Look out for snakes," I warned them, then sprinted back into school.

With graduation almost ready to start, Mrs. Crespo was super busy, and we had to stay right next to her. First she tracked down the school custodian and told him about the mice in Georgie's locker. Then she started organizing the graduation ceremony, making Georgie walk on her right side and me on her left so we couldn't even whisper to each other. It was really embarrassing when Goon saw Mrs. Crespo holding our hands like kindergartners. But the worst thing was that I was going to have to give my sister 32 points.

These points are really important to me. I've mentioned the Point Battle before. It's my secret way of keeping track of the war between me and my sister.

She knows nothing about it. Neither does anyone else. I started it at the beginning of fourth grade, even though Goon had been mean to me for years before that. When fifth grade started, I was behind by 97 points. But by paying attention and really working at winning, I was now down by only 23 points. Remember I said that the score was 615 to 592? Giving her 32 more points for the Mouse Plot disaster would be really terrible, and I'd have to award her that many if she found out that I'd been punished.

Here's how the Point Battle is scored:

If one of us insults the other—

- When we're alone: 1 point
- When other people can hear: 2 points
- Points are doubled for a REALLY excellent insult.

If one of us causes the other to do something embarrassing—

- When we're alone: 2 points
- When other people are around: 4 points
- Points are doubled for a REALLY excellent embarrassment.

If one of us gets punished—

- By parents: 4 points
- By school: 8 points
- By police: You lose—GAME OVER

Points are doubled when . . .

- it's a REALLY BIG punishment.
- you're caught lying.
- the other kid tattles.
- the other kid is actually at fault but gets
  away unpunished.

Sometimes figuring out the points can be very complicated.

Try this one. What if I smash Goon with a really excellent insult when no one is around, and she gets so mad that she throws a book at me and breaks a window, and then when Mom finds out, Goon claims that I broke the glass, and Mom believes her and punishes me?

That would be 1 point for me for the insult, doubled to 2 because of excellence, 4 for Goon because I got punished, doubled to 8 because she tattled, and doubled again to 16 because it was really her fault. Total: 14 points for Goon.

No one gets any points if the other kid doesn't know that anything happened.

So, because holding Mrs. Crespo's hand was really embarrassing, Goon was certainly going to get 8 points. That was bad enough. But if she found out I was actually being punished by being kept out of the fifth-grade party, I would have to add 8 more, making 16. And because she was the one who ratted on our Mouse Plot, I'd have to double it to 32 points.

(I think "ratted on our Mouse Plot" is funny. If you know any other excellent rodent jokes, please go to my website and tell me. I'm building a collection of them, and maybe I can add yours.)

Since I'm the only one who decides what points to give, I could, if I wanted to, give myself points all the time. Goon looked at me weird: 3 points. Goon was

mean to me: 9 points. Goon whatever: 88 points! But why would I bother to keep track of the Point Battle score if I could win whenever I wanted? I keep a fair and accurate score. I'm very serious about it.

My goal is to be ahead of Goon when she finally stops picking on me. I don't know when that will be . . . if ever. So the Point Battle could go on forever. No matter how long it lasts, I intend to win.

The graduation ceremony finally started. When we marched into the room, I could see Gumpy and Meemo sitting with my parents and Granpa. Mom, Gumpy, and Meemo were smiling. Dad and Granpa were giving me the squinty-evil-eye. I was too miserable to squinty-evil-eye back.

Mrs. Crespo made Georgie and me change from our assigned seats and sit right in the very first row where she could keep an eye on us. "If you behave," she said, "I will not mention this to your parents."

The class and everyone else recited the Pledge of Allegiance. Georgie did not cross his eyes.

Boring.

We sang "This Land Is Your Land." Georgie did not hold his breath and did not turn bright red.

Boring.

Mrs. Crespo gave her speech. Georgie did not pretend to throw up on Lana Shen, who because we had changed seats wasn't sitting anywhere near us. But even if she had been next to Georgie . . . no way.

Boring.

We listened to Francine Binki recite her poem. Georgie did not slide slowly out of his chair.

Boring.

We got our diplomas. And finally, when Alex Welch walked past, grinning at us and humming "Three Blind Mice," Georgie did not trip him. He really wanted to. I saw his leg start to move. But he stopped himself.

Boring.

It was almost noon. All I could think about was our fifth-grade party. The grassy field behind the school was going to be converted into a huge water park with sprinklers, Slip 'N Slides, water balloon games, and all kinds of desserts. We were supposed to go home, have lunch, then change into our swimsuits and come back to school at three o'clock.

Georgie, his face super mad, whispered to me, "If Mrs. Crespo doesn't let us have fun at the party, this is going to be the worst day of my life."

I nodded, looking at Mrs. Crespo to make sure she hadn't seen Georgie whispering.

"And it's all your sister's fault." His angry voice got a little bit louder.

Mrs. Crespo, who was at the microphone making a final announcement about the party, turned toward us. I coughed very loudly, masking Georgie's final comment.

"We abso . . . (COUGH-COUGH-COUGH) . . . revenge."

Finally it was over, and my parents and grand-parents swarmed over me with hugs and kisses.

"A buck for each grade," Gumpy said as he slipped a five-dollar bill into my pocket.

I mumbled a thank-you.

"Why were you in the front row out of alphabetical order?" Dad asked.

Mrs. Crespo overheard him.

"Hello, Caldwell," she said with a big grin. That's my dad's real name, but almost everyone calls him Cal. He told me that when he was in Mrs. Crespo's fourth-grade class, everyone called him Dweller, which I think is a very cool nickname. When I was in fourth grade, I called my father Dweller instead of Dad for almost the whole year. He kind of liked it, but after a while I quit. I guess I liked having a Dad better than a Dweller.

"Ronald and George were quite cooperative just before the ceremony," she said, patting me on the head, "so I rewarded them with a front-row seat." She looked right at me and Georgie. "I know you're going to have fun at the party." Then—*I swear this is true*—she gave my father a squinty-evil-eye, and he gave one back!

Just then Goon walked by with Kevin Welch. "Your teacher has asked us to be in charge of games at your party," she said with a smirky look. Normally the thought that Goon was going to be at *my* party would have really made me mad. But not this time. I grinned at her. My boring graduation was over. Mrs. Crespo, the used-to-be-youngest, squinty-evil-eyed-funniest, maybe-still-shortest, definitely-not-strictest principal, had not PARTIALLY EXPELLED us. Therefore, Goon was getting only 8 points instead of 32.

The score was now 623 to 592.

Chapter 7

The Most Bloodthirsty Vampire in Massachusetts

"How—howdy-how—howdy-how-how did we NOT get punished?" Georgie yelled to me as we biked toward home.

"Me neither!" I shouted.

"Me neither" may sound like a goofy answer, but it's really not. Because if Georgie knew the answer, he wouldn't have asked the question, and since I didn't know the answer either, saying "Me neither" was actually a good shortcut.

Georgie and I have a lot of shortcuts. It's one of the things I like about having a best friend.

"Race you home!" I yelled. I waited for him to get even with me, then began pedaling full blast. You might think that Georgie, who is bigger and stronger than I am, could ride faster. Well, he can't. When he pedals fast, his weight shifts from side to side, and his handlebars wobble, so he loses speed. But I am fast and steady.

I am also an excellent breather. When you are doing something like running or fast bicycling, you will do much, much better if you take really deep breaths instead of lots of short ones. My dad says it's because deep breaths open your lungs wider and more oxygen gets into your blood and muscles. When you're racing, it's hard to take deep breaths because your body really wants to do the short ones. But if you force yourself to fill your lungs up, you won't get tired as quickly. You should try it. It works.

So I usually win our bike races, except when, because my bike needs a tune-up, I shift too fast and my chain falls off. And this time I was leading big when I turned onto Eureka Avenue.

I skidded to a stop, breathing hard. Graduation and the Mouse Plot had made me forget all about The Haunted Toad.

About two hours later (I'm kidding . . . I wasn't *that* far ahead), Georgie skidded next to me. We both stared up at the curtained windows.

"What (pant)?" Georgie panted.

"We (pant) have to knock (pant) on the door (pant)," I panted back.

Georgie shook his head. "Why (pant)?"

When my breathing had gone back to normal, I reminded him about the heart necklace and the coin. "Eureka. Remember? The phone book says G. J. Prott lives here. We should tell him what we found."

"You said 'him,'" Georgie said. "What if G. J. Prott isn't a man? G. J. Prott might be"—his voice got all whispery—"a vampire."

Then I went "ow-hooo-eeeee" in a long, scary way, and both of us grinned at each other. Of course I do not really believe in vampires. Here's why:

1. If vampires were real, some lady—in
   movies it's mostly women who get bitten by
   vampires—would maybe have lived to tell
   about being attacked, and she would have

bite marks on her neck, and she would make lots of money being on TV and showing her bite scars and telling the whole scary story.

2. I have never seen a vampire.

3. No one I know has ever seen a vampire.

4. No one I know knows anyone who knows anyone who has ever seen a vampire. (If you have seen a vampire or, even better, been bitten by one, please go to my website and tell me. You might become famous!)

"We can write a note to G. J. Prott," I decided, "and leave it here on our way back to the party."

"Good idea," Georgie said, and zoomed off on his bike. When he was two houses away, he shouted, "Race you home!"

"Cheater!" I yelled, and took off after him.

As we rode away, there was a flutter of curtains across The Haunted Toad's upstairs windows, as if something large had flown from room to room. Then one of the curtains parted and a hideous face, dripping blood from its monstrous fangs, peered out as we disappeared down the block. It was Geejape Rott, the

Geejape Rott... d[o]
mess with this vam[p]

most evil, most dangerous, most bloodthirsty vampire
in Massachusetts.

* * *

What's wrong with the paragraph above?

First, how could I see the vampire if I was pedaling
super fast after Georgie the Cheater? And how would I
know that Geejape Rott (cool name for a vampire, IMO)
is the *most* awful vampire in Massachusetts unless I
knew about all the other vampires in Massachusetts?

And besides, there are no vampires in Massachusetts.

I just wanted to write something really scary. Maybe my next book will be all about vampires.

Or zombies.

* * *

With only three houses to go until we got to my driveway, I had caught up to Georgie the Cheater. But he must have been saving his strength or something, because when he saw me out of the corner of his eye, he put out a blast of pedaling power, and I lost by a front wheel.

"Cheater (gasp)!" I gasped as I leaned my bike up against my garage.

Georgie grinned and did a goofy victory dance holding up the front wheel of his bike. I hate cheating. Here's why:

1. Let's say you're the second-shortest kid in your class and you're always playing games with kids who are way bigger than you. Sure, you might lose a lot, but you'll never know how good you really are at these games if you cheat.

2. Let's say you're the biggest kid in your class and there's only one sports thing—bike riding—that your best friend is better at than you. Do you have to cheat at that one thing so you'll be best at everything?

3. Cheating makes you weak. (Granpa told me this.) Cheaters don't have to work as hard to win, so they do not get as strong or as good.

Like I said when I was describing the Point Battle in Chapter 6, I don't cheat.

Georgie was grinning. I was not. He stopped his cheater dance, stared at me, and finally gave in. "Okay, calm down. The race doesn't count."

"Ronnie!" my mother shouted from somewhere inside our house.

"What?" I yelled back.

"Come in for lunch!" she barked.

"What'd you make?" I screamed.

"Tuna salad sandwiches!" she hollered.

"In a while!" I growled.

"Come in now!" she howled.

"I'm eating at Georgie's!" I roared. (Georgie and I

eat together about four or five times a week, so a long time ago we agreed that we don't have to ask permission to eat at the other guy's house. It's kind of a best friend bonus.)

"Change your clothes first!" Mom shrieked.

(There must be about a hundred different words that tell how someone talks. This conversation could have gone on lots longer and I still wouldn't have run out! I especially like the word *guffaw*, which I think means to laugh loudly with your mouth wide open. I have not yet had a chance to use it in this book, but I will!)

Georgie leaned his bike against mine. "See you at my house," he said, and trotted into my backyard toward the won't-close-gate.

I ran up to my room and grabbed my swimsuit and a towel. Then I stashed the graduation five-dollar bill from Gumpy in my backpack—my mom says that you should always have some money with you in case of emergencies—and ran downstairs. But I got waylaid (great word—my dad says it's what ambushers do) by the huge collection of grandparents in my living room.

The first to stop me was Gumpy, who teaches computers and stuff at Yale College. He asked about my Little League team. He loves baseball but never plays ball with me because he is a terrible thrower because he was shot in the shoulder in the Vietnam War. I've seen the scar. But he refuses to tell me any gory details about it even though I have asked him a million times.

I told him that my Little League team came in last, but I batted .383, mostly singles, and stole 22 bases. He nodded, then tapped the tips of his fingers and thumbs together, which is like what Mrs. Crespo does, except that it means he is going to give me a math problem, which he does every time he sees me because he is very good at math and knows I am, too.

"Let's say (tap, tap) there's eighty-three cents in my pocket," he said. "What's the fewest number of coins I could have?"

"United States coins?" I asked.

He nodded (tap, tap).

I thought for a few seconds and answered, "Four."

His forehead wrinkled up like he was surprised at

me. "Nope. Six. A half-dollar, a quarter, a nickel, and three pennies."

But I proved I was right . . . and he was amazed.

This is not a trick question. If you don't know why four is the correct answer, look around in this book. I stuck a clue in. And if you give up, I put the answer on my website: CheesieMack.com.

My next obstacle was Meemo, who is the champion kisser and hugger of my whole family. I usually don't mind because I love her, and she is a very excellent baker of chocolate-chip cookies. She gave me one of her famous Meemo Monster Hugs and shoved me over to the laundry-room door, where parents and grandparents have been marking off how tall Goon and I are since we were babies. Then Meemo had to find a book to level my head with. Then she had to find a pencil. Then she marked a new line on the door. Then she had to call my mother over to show her that I had only grown a half-inch since Christmas, and was I getting enough protein in my diet? All this time she was holding my hand so I could not get away.

But finally Granpa rescued me. He sort of dragged

me into the hallway and began telling me all the reasons why I should go to camp:

He said, "Camp will be fun."

I said, "Not without Georgie."

He said, "I'll need your help with the Little Guys."

I said, "I wish I could, but I promised."

He said, "Camp starts in three weeks, and you'll want to see your friends."

I said, "I'm staying here. Georgie's my best friend."

Granpa didn't nod or smile or anything, but he gave me a squinty-evil-eye. I think it meant that he understood what it means to have a best friend.

I ran out the back door with Deeb racing after me, but she stopped at the gully. I have trained her not to leave our backyard unless I give her a specific command.

When I walked into Georgie's kitchen, Mr. Sinkoff was putting tuna salad sandwiches onto three plates. Of course I instantly knew that Georgie, after listening to my mother, had gotten hungry for tuna salad sandwiches and asked his father to make some.

One of the things about having best friends is that lots of times you know exactly what they're going to do. It's kind of like mind reading. For example, Georgie can always tell when I'm lying. About a year ago he figured out that when I lie, I blink my eyes a lot. When he told me, I tried to stop blinking. Not that I lie a lot. I'm not a perfect kid or anything, but my lying was mostly happening when I was trying to play a joke on someone, not when I was trying to hide being bad or anything. But when you find out for sure that your eyes give you away like blinking signs that say "I'm a liar! I'm a liar!" you better not lie too much. So I don't.

I called, and Georgie trotted downstairs, picked up our plates, and ran up the stairs. I picked up our two glasses of milk and followed. I did not run. It is stupid to run up stairs with milk.

Georgie closed the door to his room behind me. He chomped a gigantic bite out of his sandwich and tuna-mouthed, "Gross-out contest!"

Chewing loudly with his mouth wide open, he lifted his sandwich up for another huge bite, so I smooshed it into his face with the palm of my hand and guffawed, "You win!"

(My advice: Use *guffaw* in your school writing. Your teacher will love it!)

Georgie is a good sport. He grinned and wiped his face on a T-shirt that was lying on his bed. He had forgotten to bring napkins upstairs.

I wiped my hands on my socks.

I got the sock idea exactly when I invented the BLART sandwich—that's Bacon-Lettuce-Avocado-Ranch dressing-Tomato. Excellent and tasty, but very messy! The first time I took a bite out of side 1, gunk squished out of side 2, side 3, and side 4. My hands

 were dripping, and I didn't have a napkin or anything. But I had socks, so I used them. No one has ever noticed me wiping my fingers on my ankle, and no one can tell if I have white ranch dressing smeared on white socks. I think ketchup and mustard would be really obvious, however, so make sure you have a napkin or red and yellow socks if you're eating hot dogs or hamburgers.

(The reason I'm telling all this about BLART sandwiches is because I am eating a BLART sandwich

right now, exactly while I'm writing this chapter! And it is actually a terrible idea because my computer now has a BLART-smeared mouse.)

"We need to write a note to G. J. Prott," I said.

Georgie picked up the heart necklace and the 1909 Lincoln Head penny (I mean "cent"). They had been sitting on his desk since the last time we'd been in his room. "If this Prott guy really wants this stuff back, maybe we'll get a reward. Maybe ten dollars."

"Maybe twenty," I said, smiling. I was still thinking the coin was worth three dollars.

What a dope!

Chapter 8
A Butt-Banging Escape

I set my milk down on Georgie's desk and picked up some lined paper and a pencil. I wrote:

Dear Mr. G. J. Prott,

Georgie pointed at the paper. "What if it's a woman?"

I erased and wrote:

Dear Mr. or Mrs. G. J. Prott,

"What if she's not married?" He had a little smile on his face because he knew that I knew he was right. So I erased again and wrote:

Dear Mr. or Mrs. or Ms. G. J. Prott,

"What about vampires?" Georgie asked, leaning over me and baring what he thinks are his fangs but are actually just pointed canine teeth that stick out a bit. (*Canine* means "doglike." If you want to know which are your canine teeth, just look at your dog or any dog. The biggest, sharpest ones . . . those are canines. In humans, too. How do I know this stuff about teeth? I have a very talkative dentist.)

Georgie has braces on his teeth, so that even with his sharp canines, he looks like a kid with metal in his mouth. He is not the least bit vampirish. I ignored him and continued writing:

Dear Mr. or Mrs. or Ms. G. J. Prott,
   We found an old envelop that was mailed to

"You misspelled *envelope*," Georgie said.
"Did not," I replied. "It doesn't have to have an *e*

at the end. It can be spelled either way. You can look it up. Anyway, I left the *e* off on purpose so our note would be more mysterious."

"Lame," Georgie muttered.

Just to please him, I stuck the *e* back in.

Actually I did look *envelop* up, and darn it, Georgie was right. The two words are pronounced differently: *envelop* = en-VEH-lop, but *envelope* = EN-veh-lope. They also have different meanings. I found an explanation on a college website, Canada's University of Victoria:

> *Envelop* is a verb meaning "to surround" and is most frequently used to describe fog or a mother's arms. The only thing an *envelope* surrounds is a letter.

I could have left this *envelop/envelope* stuff out, but like I said, I don't cheat, even if it means I lose. And anyway, Georgie, who never gets excellent grades in spelling, is reading this over my shoulder while I'm writing, and he is insisting I leave it in.

Here's what the note looked like when it was finished:

Dear Mr. or Mrs. or Ms. G. J. Prott,
   We found an old envelope that was
mailed to you about 50 years ago when
you lived at 39 Sutcliffe Street. There
was something in it.
                    Yours truly,
                    Georgie Sinkoff (who lives
                    in your old house)
                    Ronald Mack (who lives in the
                    house just on the other side of
                    the creek behind your old house)

"And we need to have a way to get an answer,"
Georgie added.

He was right again, so I added something at the
bottom:

   P.S.—If you want to know what we
   found, please leave us an answer on
   your front porch.

When I looked up from my writing, Georgie had

gotten into his swimsuit and tucked his towel and clothes into a backpack.

I put the necklace and the penny back into the old envelope—I didn't put the folded paper in with them because Georgie had burned one corner and smudged pencil lead on it. I grabbed my backpack and put the Prott note and the old envelope in it.

"We have three important things to do this afternoon," I said as I changed into my swimsuit. "First, we drop off the note. Second, we go to the party and have fun. Third, and most important, we figure out how to get back at my tattletale sister."

The day was warm and sunny, perfect for the outdoor school party. As we biked toward The Haunted Toad, we decided that I would deliver the note because I am the fastest runner, and Georgie would hold our bikes.

When we got to Eureka Avenue, a police car drove past us.

"Don't worry, he's just on patrol," Georgie said.

I looked at him quizzically (another word Dad

taught me). "Why should we be worried? We aren't going to break any laws, so we don't have to worry about being worried."

Even so, we waited until the patrol car disappeared around the corner, then rode up the street and stopped next to a bunch of trash cans between The Haunted Toad and the next house. We got off and stood staring at the old green-gray building.

"Someone . . . or something . . . is watching us," I whispered.

"Vampires, probably," Georgie replied softly.

I knew he was kidding, but as I looked up at the old house, even though everything looked just like it always had, I had the feeling that it was different.

"Come on!" Georgie whispered loudly. "You want me to do it?"

I glared at him. "I'll do it. You just hold my bike and be ready to pedal fast!"

I waited until another car drove by, then squinched (I made this word up . . . it means squeezing along inch by inch) through some bushes at the end of the front fence and began sneaking soundlessly across the front yard like a ninja or an Indian stalking a deer.

(Granpa, who thinks he knows all about Indians and forests and stuff because he's director of our summer camp, once told me, "No one, not Cochise or Sitting Bull or the Last of the Mohicans, could walk on leaves and twigs without crunching." Granpa: When you read this, please believe me. There were plenty of twigs, leaves, and other junk on The Haunted Toad's lawn, but I walked with absolutely no crunching noise. It *can* be done!)

I leaned on the railing as I climbed the three front steps, so that my weight on the stairs would be very light and maybe they wouldn't squeak.

They didn't squeak.

I put the folded note in the crack where the door opens, pounded twice on the door, and ran full blast for my bike.

(Granpa: Don't ask. I admit to lots of crunching on the way back.)

Our getaway was not as smooth as we had planned. Here's why:

1. I caught my shirt on a bush when I ran back.

2. That sort of spun me sideways so that I sort of stumbled into my bike.

3. My bike fell against Georgie.

4. Georgie lost his balance, fell backward, and banged his behind against the trash barrel.

5. The trash barrel, which was full of bottles and cans for recycling, spilled into the street. Bottles broke, making a lot of noise.

6. We jumped on our bikes and pumped hard, but about three houses down the block, I speed-shifted and my chain came off the sprocket.

7. Running alongside my bike, I chased after Georgie, who had stopped when he noticed that I wasn't anywhere near.

Even with our bumbling, bungled, butt-banging, bike-breaking escape, we were eight houses down the block and almost out of sight before anyone could've come to the door of The Haunted Toad. I flipped my bike upside down and began speedily reattaching the chain.

(I like the word *speedily*. It's one of those words that sounds like what it means . . . at least to me. Some others are *gargoyle*—sounds monstrous and evil;

lizard—sounds scaly and fast-moving; and *carnival*—sounds bouncy and fun. I am building a collection of words like this on my website. If you want to add one to my list—and I don't mean obvious words that imitate sounds like *buzz* or *plop* or *fizzle*—please go to my website.)

I had just righted my bike when that police car passed us going back toward The Haunted Toad. Georgie spun his bike around, straddled it, and looked at the car. About a second later, I did, too.

The squad car continued until it was just about even with The Haunted Toad, then stopped in the middle of the street.

"What's he doing?" I wondered out loud.

"Come on!" Georgie said, riding away.

Before I could follow, a woman (G. J. Prott?) stepped onto the sidewalk and waved her arms at the police car. When she pointed in our direction, it was as if that arm froze me. I couldn't move.

The police car U-turned and drove up right next to me. The policeman stared without speaking. He looked angry or mean or both. He turned toward

Georgie, who was two houses away, stuck an arm out the patrol car's window, and motioned. Georgie rode back and stopped next to me.

When the policeman finally spoke, his voice was scratchy and odd. "I know you. I know both of you."

The Labyrinthine Terture Chamber Dungeen

I, Ronal Dwellerson, cannot remember our capture. I now think it was a witfog spell that overcame us. We had been completely unprepared, standing beside our wheelers, unarmed and unarmored, surprised by one of Peezoff Fizzur's black four-rollers . . . and then there was nothing . . . until the dark became more than just blackness, and Geo and I, tethered by metal chains, were stumbling over the uneven stone floor, pulled by a massive horned creature.

In the smoky light of rimtorches, we could see only the rock tunnel walls and the hide of the monster's back, matted and marred with what must have been dried blood and the knotted scars of old wounds. He

stopped at a heavy wooden door and pushed it open, revealing a very small, very damp room. Then he turned to face us. A thick brass spiral sharpened at both ends hung from his belt, and a long thread of snot from his nose.

"I know you," he said in a reedy voice so wrong. "I know both of you."

* * *

Remember I wrote Chapter 4α in science-fiction style? Well, just when I started to write about the policeman and me and Georgie, my sister, in her room with one of her friends, began to blah-blah-blah *way too loudly* about why Harry Potter was better than Narnia and Frodo. So I decided to write what happened to me and Georgie as if we were living in Middle Earth or Narnwarts. My dad helped me with some of the sentences.

I think Ronal Dwellerson is a very cool name. And maybe Georgie would like to be called Geo. I'm going to ask him.

Anyway, you get the idea. And that's why this is Chapter 8§.

(I don't know what that squiggle is. I just found it on my computer and decided it looked old and magical.)

Maybe someday I'll write a fantasy book.

Chapter 9
Busted by the Cops

I am sure you have heard this: If you fall off a cliff and are plunging toward the jagged rocks below, your whole life will flash through your mind in the split second before you die.

Well, that's sort of what happened to me in the split second after the policeman spoke. Here's what went through my mind:

1. I want to pet my dog. (Makes sense. I love Deeb. But why did I think of this first?)

2. Even after I was forced to hold Mrs. Crespo's hand at graduation, now I'm going to miss my graduation party. (Makes sense. I really wanted to go.)

3. In first grade I wet my pants at recess once,

and my teacher never told my mother. (I don't know why I thought of this, and it's a little embarrassing, but it really flashed through my mind, so I won't leave it out.)

4. E-I-E-I-O. (What was this all about? It even had the music to it. Sometimes I don't understand how my mind works.)

5. Point Battle. Go to jail. GAME OVER. Goon wins. (After all the other thoughts evaporated, this was all that was left . . . and it was really loud.)

The policeman got out of his car and walked toward us. He was tall and very big, like a football player. He had a gun in a holster on his belt. The belt had lots of gadgets and bullets and stuff on it. He had a badge on his chest and a name tag that said "Crompton." He looked at Georgie for a long time.

"Either of you boys . . ." He paused and looked at me with hard, staring eyes. "Know anything about what happened . . ." He turned his head toward Georgie, but his eyes stayed on me. "Back there?" He pointed very slowly toward The Haunted Toad.

I looked back up the road toward the house. The woman was still there, staring back. I looked at Georgie. His eyebrows were waggling up and down. I knew that if I didn't speak, Georgie would start talking, and when he did, he'd blab everything. So I started talking first.

"We didn't really do anything wrong. I mean, okay, maybe we did. I don't know all the laws. You probably do, being a police officer and stuff. But we had this note to deliver, and we didn't want to bother the person who lived there, so we, I mean I—Georgie didn't because he was holding my bike—went across The Haunted Toad's lawn. That's what we call that old green house, not because we think it's actually haunted or it's a toad or anything like that. We just think that's what it looks like. And I know I didn't ruin or break anything. Okay, maybe a branch of a bush—I got my shirt caught, and it was a little branch. Really little. But we had this note to deliv—"

It was at this point I realized that I was doing exactly what I wanted to keep Georgie from doing. So I shut up.

The policeman was an excellent starer.

Finally he said, "You're Cal Mack's son, aren't you?"

How did he know? I gulped, then nodded.

"And you." He turned to Georgie. "You're Ben Sinkoff's boy, right?"

Knows every kid in Gloucester!

Georgie's nod was so small, the policeman just kept staring until Georgie nodded a second time, much bigger.

"Why don't you two just ride your bikes back up the block and park in front of that green house? I'll be right behind you."

We rode very slowly. The police car followed very slowly.

"We're going to jail," Georgie whispered loudly.

I swallowed really hard. My knees were shaking all by themselves. "How does he know who we are?"

As we approached The Haunted Toad, the woman on the sidewalk never took her eyes off us.

I whispered, "She must be G. J. Prott."

We parked our bikes and stood next to them. The

woman looked really mad, but she didn't say anything until Officer Crompton got out of the police car and walked over. Then she began waving her arms every which way and bawling us out. "Thispolicemanjust happenedtobedrivingbyandsuchamesswhatgives youtwotroublemakersmygoodness?"

She was so upset that her words all ran together, and I had no idea what she was talking about. She was waving one arm and pointing with the other at the tipped-over recycling barrel. Then she spun around and pointed at the white house next to The Haunted Toad and said, "TenyearsI'velivedherepeaceful neighborhoodthisismytrashcansodisgracefulandifyou thinkI'mgoingtowellyou'rewrong."

I looked at the house she was pointing toward. I was completely confused. Then suddenly it hit me.

I started grinning. Georgie looked at me like I was crazy. Then I burst out laughing.

The lady stopped waving her arms.

Officer Crompton's stern look got even sterner.

"We are sooooo," I managed to croak through my laughter, "sorry." I started bouncing on the balls of my feet. This lady wasn't G. J. Prott! She was G. J. Prott's next-door neighbor, and Georgie and I were guilty of littering!

Guffawing (there's that word again!) and choking, I grabbed Georgie and pulled him over to the tipped trash barrel and its scattered pile of bottles and cans. I was hooting and ha-hooing as I picked up the barrel. I was hey-harring and ho-heeing as I grabbed an empty wine bottle and a couple of crushed soda cans and tossed them in. Then Georgie got the idea and bounded into action. He snatched up wine bottles in both hands, stood, spun, and did a jumping double-stuff into the barrel. We became bathing-suited zoom chucklers.

(I just made that up, but I'm sure you know what I mean.)

It took us no time at all to pick up everything except the bottles that had broken into lots of glass pieces.

The policeman hadn't moved or said a word while we were cleaning up. "Don'ttouch," the woman warned. "I'llgetabroom."

"We are so sorry," I repeated, this time without

giggling. I turned to Officer Crompton. "May we leave? We have to get to our graduation party."

He nodded.

I said, "May I ask you a question?"

The policeman stared.

"How do you know who we are?"

"I know every kid in Gloucester," he said with a thin smile. "So watch yourself."

Officer Crompton then pointed to the lady's house and The Haunted Toad and said, "No more trash can problems. No more notes. I want you two boys to stay away from these houses, you hear?"

Georgie and I nodded seriously, and the policeman walked back toward his car. As we got on our bikes, I looked back at The Haunted Toad. The note I had stuck in the door was gone!

Chapter 10
Class Party Trickery

All the other fifth graders were already at school having fun when we arrived. The playground had been transformed into a water park . . . kind of. Two of the sprinklers were on, a big waterslide had been set up, and there was a huge Slip 'N Slide mat on the hill by the side fence. Everybody was wet and almost everybody was yelling or squealing.

As we walked through the gate, two boys in our class heaved water balloons at us. They missed, and Ms. Higgins, our mostly terrific teacher, warned them she was going to be setting up the dessert table, and it was off-limits to water balloons. "So cool it right now!" Goon and her supposed boyfriend Kevin Welch, whom I do not like, were sitting at the table.

I ignored them and walked toward the playground.

About one minute later, nearly all the boys and a few of the girls were gathered around us listening to how Georgie and I were almost just arrested for littering. Georgie waved his arms all around like G. J. Prott's neighbor lady while I told the story. Everybody seemed shocked when we told them that Officer Crompton knows every kid in town by sight, except for Glenn Philips, who said that with over four thousand kids in Gloucester schools, "Such a feat of memory is entirely unlikely." Then Mrs. Crespo told Georgie and me to get our tickets for the drawing because the prize would be forty dollars' worth of pizza and stuff at the best pizza place in town.

We went over to the dessert table, where Ms. Higgins was putting out the goodies. Kevin and Goon sat at the end. He was holding the roll of red tickets for the party's prize drawing. She was just sitting. He tore off two tickets, removed our stubs and set them on the table, and handed our tickets to us. My number was 05554. Georgie looked at his ticket, got excited, and then stuck

it in my face and pointed at the number. It was one more than mine, and he was excited about all the fives. He showed it to Kevin and hooted.

Kevin said, "Don't get all bonko. You're gonna lose."

"Maybe not, maybe not." Georgie grinned. "I'm very lucky, and this is a very lucky number."

"Not today, you're not," Kevin said. He looked at Goon, who nodded, made a big L with her thumb and pointer finger, and said, "Loser."

Georgie is not afraid of bigger kids. He glared at Kevin.

Kevin sneered a grinning sneer and picked up our two ticket stubs. He handed them to Goon, who made a big show of stuffing them through the slot in the lid of the jar that held all the other stubs for the drawing, but I saw what she really did.

Yeah, I saw what she did, and I thought about the Point Battle and how this might be my big chance. I thought about this for a few seconds, but because of all the fun going on, I did not think about it again for the next ninety minutes. Here's what I did instead:

1. I ran around like a lunatic. No one could catch me. Lana Shen is the only kid who is faster than I am, but she didn't even try.

2. I ate three colossal scoops of ice cream on one cone—brown cow, double fudge, and mint chip. There were six different kinds to choose from. You can probably guess that I love chocolate.

3. I did an awesomely dangerous trick that ended with a terrific face-plant in the mud. Everyone cheered! Ms. Higgins commanded me not to do it again.

4. I ate five strings of red licorice in less than one minute. Georgie dared me. I dared him back, and he ate nine and almost threw up!

5. I took a huge running start, then scoogled (this is my made-up word . . . it is a combination of *scoot* and *wiggle*) on the Slip 'N Slide and skivolvunged butt-first into the dirt, which was actually mud. (Can you guess what *skivolvunged* is a three-way combo of? The answer is on my website.)

6. I ate one bite of a homemade, low-fat, low-sugar, organic oatmeal-raisin-carob cookie that Ms. Higgins made. IMO the real ingredients were cat litter, library paste, wood chunks, and rabbit pellets, so I fed the rest to Mrs. Crespo's pug dog, who is so ugly he is cute.

7. I invented a game that almost the whole class played. I named it Playground Marco Polo, and it's just like in a swimming pool except everyone bumps around on their knees. It doesn't have to be in mud, but ours was.

8. I split two double-stick Popsicles—one orange and one green—with Georgie. The combination turned our tongues brown.

I had as much fun as any kid in the world could possibly have in ninety minutes on a warm, sunny June day on a sopping-wet public school playground in Gloucester, Massachusetts.

Then Ms. Higgins called out for everyone to gather for the prize drawing. Mrs. Crespo stood smiling as Goon and Kevin handed her the jar of ticket stubs.

As soon as I saw the jar, I instantly knew what I was going to do. I grabbed Georgie's shoulder and whispered, "Today, at our graduation, my sister tattled on us. Sure, we were guilty in the Mouse Plot, but that's not the point. She ratted on us and almost got us Partially Expelled. But now we get our revenge."

Georgie had no idea what I was planning to do, but he grinned anyway. He's my best friend.

"Boys and girls," Mrs. Crespo announced, "it's time for the prize drawing. Get your tickets." Everybody ran to their backpacks, which is where we were told to stash our tickets during the water party.

Alex Welch pulled his ticket out of his bathing suit pocket and whined, "I can't read my number. It's all soggy." Kevin laughed at his little brother and called him a dope. Ms. Higgins patted Alex on the head.

Alex rewhined, "I need another ticket."

Ms. Higgins gave Alex a stop-the-whining face, and he shut up.

"Give me yours," I said softly to Georgie.

"Why?" he whispered back, holding out his ticket.

"Just watch," I said, taking it from him.

Mrs. Crespo, smiling broadly and standing tall—which for her is still very, very short—proclaimed, "I shall now, after a proper shaking to assure random mixing . . ." She shook the jar of stubs. ". . . draw out a single ticket." She unscrewed the lid. "And we shall then have a winner of the forty-dollar pizza party, to which I hope I will be invited, because I do like pizza so very much."

I read somewhere that pizza is the favorite food of American kids. I don't know if that is actually true. Whenever I travel, I see way more hamburger signs than pizza signs. But pizza is my personal favorite. If you want to vote on your favorite food, please go to my website—CheesieMack.com—and let me know your opinion.

Mrs. Crespo held up the jar of ticket stubs and started to reach in for a ticket, but I jumped forward and interrupted. "Mrs. Crespo! Before you draw a winner, I have a question."

She raised her eyebrows in a yes-what-is-it way.

"Is this supposed to be a fair and honest drawing?" I asked.

She looked surprised. "Of course."

I walked toward her. "And if you found out that someone had cheated, would the cheater be punished?"

"Certainly."

"And what if the cheater was someone you had put your trust in, someone who abused that trust?" I was now standing near the dessert table, right next to Goon.

"The punishment would be severe." She had now set the jar back on the dessert table. "Do you have something to tell me, Ronald?"

"Yes. Yes, I do. Here are the tickets that Kevin Welch and my sister gave to me and Georgie when we got here." I held our bright red tickets up for everyone to see. "In order for this to be fair and honest, the people who gave us these tickets would have put our stubs in that jar with all the other stubs. Right?"

Mrs. Crespo looked impatient.

"But my sister and her accomplice, Kevin Welch, have purposely and cheatingly made certain that

Georgie and I would not have the tiniest chance of winning by hiding our stubs in her pocket!"

If I have done a good job of describing, you will realize that this moment was like a scene from one of those television shows where the good-guy lawyer, Mr. R. Cheshire MacAronie, Esq., has just sprung a clever trap on the villains, the master criminal known as Madame Goon and her muscle-bound sidekick, Kevin the Welcher. As a result of MacAronie's superb cunning, the malevolent (muh-LEH-voh-lent, which means "really evil") villains are trapped, caught,

pinned, and exposed in front of the entire courtroom of witnesses—in this case, my fifth-grade class, my teacher, and my principal.

Mrs. Crespo turned to my sister. "June?"

"My brother is an idiot. I did no such thing."

"I saw her do it," I said.

"I don't have your stupid stubs. Idiot."

"That's enough, June. I'll handle this." Mrs. Crespo began tapping her fingers together. Tapping fingers meant, you remember, that guilt was already decided and punishment was coming. I was doomed. This would be a big loss in the Point Battle. Big. My face felt hot. Everyone was looking at me.

"After this morning's events—you do recall the incident I am referring to?—I thought we had an understanding about your behavior, Ronald. But it appears that I was wrong. I shall have to—"

Suddenly I blurted out, "Empty her pockets!" And then I yelled, "MAKE HER EMPTY HER POCKETS!"

I looked at Goon. Her hand started to reach toward her back pocket . . . then stopped.

Sometimes you do something without thinking. That's what I did right then. I leaped at Goon, grabbing her around the waist and reaching for her back pockets.

We struggled.

She pushed.

I thrashed.

I heard yelling—probably me and Mrs. Crespo and Georgie and everybody else, but I couldn't tell one noise from the other.

Goon, who is bigger and stronger than I am, jabbed out with the heel of her hand and caught me in the mouth. I tasted blood, but I was so focused on finding those ticket stubs that nothing hurt.

Goon kicked me. I didn't even feel it.

"Stop fighting!" Mrs. Crespo yelled, grabbing us both and shoving us apart. "This is—"

Panting almost uncontrollably, I interrupted. "Punish me! Punish me if I'm wrong! But if I'm right, then you have to look in her pockets."

Mrs. Crespo was unconvinced.

"Please!" I pleaded. "If the ticket stubs aren't

there, then my sister is right, and I *am* an idiot, and whatever punishment you were going to give me, double it!"

Mrs. Crespo looked straight at me, one eye getting slitty because she was thinking so hard. It looked just like she was giving me the squinty-evil-eye, but without anything funny in it. Everyone was silent. Right then I became aware of my split lip and tasted the blood in my mouth. I could feel my heart pounding in my temples. I looked at my sister. She hadn't moved. Her face looked frozen.

Then Georgie stepped up and said, "Punish me, too. If Cheesie's wrong, then we're *both* idiots and make it *triple*."

I told you he was my best friend.

Mrs. Crespo took a deep breath and turned toward my sister. The frozen look on Goon's face cracked into a weird sort of fake smile.

"This is ridiculous," Goon said. "I'm leaving." She started to walk away.

"Stop, young lady," Mrs. Crespo said.

Goon didn't stop.

"June!"

Goon kept walking. "Come on, Kevin," she said. Kevin ran after her, kind of like when I call Deeb.

"June!" Mrs. Crespo repeated. "I will have to call your mother."

Goon turned around suddenly, knocking into Kevin. "Please do. And tell her that my brother is a liar." She took a deep breath and calmed her voice a bit. "Mrs. Crespo, I am not trying to be disrespectful, but Ms. Higgins asked me to help, and I did, and I am just completely insulted by my brother's stupid lying." Without waiting for a response, she turned and walked away, with Kevin trotting after her.

Chapter 11
Stubs

No one said a word until Goon and Kevin were out of sight.

Finally Mrs. Crespo spoke. "Well, Miss Mack has called her brother a liar. Are you a liar, Ronald?" Her lips were pinched into a thin line. I don't think I had ever seen her so mad.

I shook my head.

"We shall see," Mrs. Crespo said as she tipped the jar of ticket stubs over onto the table. "Ms. Higgins," Mrs. Crespo said, "there are twenty-nine students at this party. Right?"

Ms. Higgins nodded.

"So," Mrs. Crespo said, "if June is correct and Ronald is lying, there should be exactly twenty-nine stubs in this pile. But if Ronald is telling the truth, there should be twenty-seven. We shall now find out."

Mrs. Crespo counted the stubs out loud and dropped them one by one back into the jar. When she reached twenty-two, I knew what the outcome would be. I could see how many stubs remained on the table.

"And the last one," Mrs. Crespo said, "makes twenty-seven. It appears, Ronald, that you are telling the truth."

"That only proves that two are missing," Glenn Philips interrupted. "To complete the proof, you need to make certain that Cheesie's and Georgie's are the ones."

Of course Glenn, who is super smart, was right.

Mrs. Crespo nodded. "What are your ticket numbers?"

Georgie answered quickly. "Mine is zero-five-five-five-five. And Cheesie's is zero-five-five-five-four."

Mrs. Crespo emptied the tickets out and dropped them back in one by one, silently scanning each for our numbers. As she dropped the last one in, she turned to Glenn. "The proof is complete." And then to me. "You are *not* a liar, Ronald."

Georgie grabbed me around the shoulders and squeezed. I grinned, and my lip hurt.

"Your sister is in big trouble now," Alex Welch said. Duh.

"And now, at last," Mrs. Crespo announced, "we shall have the pizza party drawing."

"Mrs. Crespo," Glenn interrupted, "without Cheesie's and Georgie's stubs, they can't win."

"Quite right again, Glenn," Mrs. Crespo responded. "But I have a solution. I shall now draw a winning ticket." She reached in, pulled out a ticket stub, and read the number. "Zero-five-five-three-seven." There was complete quiet for a couple of seconds while all the kids examined their tickets (except for me and Georgie).

Then Lana Shen squealed and hugged her two best friends. "I won!"

After the shrieking and screeching died down, Mrs. Crespo continued, "I will now draw for a second pizza

Pizza party winner!

party prize, identical to the first, which I will donate and which will be won by whoever has the winning ticket that I am now drawing out of this imaginary jar that contains all the missing ticket stubs."

"My ticket's sort of missing!" Alex Welch shouted. "I can't read the numbers."

Mrs. Crespo nodded at Alex, then made a big show of holding up an imaginary jar and pulling out an invisible ticket stub. "The winning number is . . . zero-five-five-five . . . and the last digit is . . . is this a four?" She pretended to peer at the imaginary ticket. "No . . . it's a five!"

"That's mine!" Georgie yelled. "Pizza!" He grabbed my shoulders and shook them really hard. "See? I told you I was lucky!"

The second winning ticket!

While Mrs. Crespo was explaining to Georgie that she would call the pizza parlor and set up his prize party and that all he had to do was call them whenever he wanted to go, I sat listening to a conversation between a dope and a genius.

"It's not fair," Alex objected.

"It is fair," Glenn explained. "Your stub was in the primary jar with all the other similar stubs."

"But the numbers were all rubbed off my ticket," Alex protested.

"Had Mrs. Crespo extracted"—Glenn really uses words like that—"your stub, you would have won, but she selected Lana's instead."

"But I couldn't read my number."

"An unmatched stub would have established your claim to the prize," Glenn explained patiently.

"But how would I know?" Alex whined.

I couldn't stand it any longer. "If she called out the number and no one claimed the prize, then the number on the stub would have to be yours!" I said directly and way too loudly into Alex's ear. Alex looked at me blankly, which is normal for him, so I gave up.

"It would be proof by the absence of evidence," Glenn continued. "Sir Arthur Conan Doyle often employs comparable methods in his Sherlock Holmes mysteries."

I have read two Sherlock Holmes stories, *The Hound of the Baskervilles* and *A Study in Scarlet*.

They are old and take place before cars and airplanes and way before computers. If you don't mind British spelling—"colours" instead of "colors"—I recommend them highly. I learned many vocabulary words from them. In fact, a few months ago, after I found the Sherlock Holmes book that I had borrowed from the library hidden inside my dog's kibble bin—it was a week overdue—I said to my father, "You may call it conjecture (guessing), but I believe that our domicile (house) is inhabited by a choleric (angry) personage (MY SISTER!) whose exploits (actions) include purloining (stealing) and deceit (lying)." My father laughed. Goon was punished. I got 8 points.

About half the class was gathered around Georgie, begging to be invited to his pizza party, while most of the others were huddled around Lana Shen, doing, I guess, the same thing. I grabbed Georgie by the back of his bathing suit and pulled him toward the Boys room.

"What's the matter?" Georgie asked once we were inside and changing out of our swimsuits.

"You better be careful how many kids you ask to your pizza party."

Georgie didn't respond. He just grabbed his wet swimsuit off the floor with his toes and flipped it backward up over his head. Georgie is a very excellent athlete. He didn't even look. He just stuck his hands out in front of him, and the suit flew over his head and landed—plop—right on them. (I cannot do this. But I have a diagram of how to do it on my website. You can try it if you want.)

"I think pizzas cost about ten bucks each. Add in drinks and you're only going to be able to buy three pies . . . maximum. Eight slices to a pie—"

Georgie was pulling on his pants, which made him lose his balance and crash into me. He is an excellent athlete, but sometimes a klutz.

I pushed him away and continued. "That's only twenty-four slices. Figuring the average kid'll eat three, maybe four slices—"

"I can eat seven," Georgie bragged.

"Yeah, but some kids'll eat only two, so that means you can invite only five or six other kids besides you and me."

"I wasn't planning to invite you," Georgie said, squatting down to tie his shoes.

I glared at him. He didn't even look back. Then I leaped onto his back and began fake-pounding him.

"You dare to insult the supreme dignity and undeniable worthiness of Dr. Cheez?! You shall be punished (pound), beaten (pound), battered (pound), and thumped mercilessly."

With me hanging on to him and continuing my fake pounding, Georgie wobbled to his feet and began lumbering around. He grunted, "Ee-Gorg sorry, Master. Ee-Gorg bad. Ee-Gorg very bad."

I already told you that Georgie is really strong and almost twice as big as I am, so a real fight would be over in less than one microsecond, with me flattened into a grease spot on the wall. So you can probably guess that this is a game Georgie and I play. In it I am the brilliant and totally warped Dr. Frank N. Cheez. Georgie is Ee-Gorg, my super-strong half-witted monster. We made up this game back in third grade, which is when he started to get really big.

When Ee-Gorg—toting his merciless, pounding master—came staggering out the bathroom door, he crashed us right into Lana Shen, who was standing there waiting. She screamed. I jumped off. Georgie, still acting like a demented (a good word to use as an insult—it means insane) monster, shambled away. Banging into everything in his path, he grunted, "Ee-Gorg get bicycle for Dr. Cheez. Ee-Gorg like bicycle. Ee-Gorg eat bicycle."

I was laughing at Georgie until I realized that Lana was standing next to me, staring and smiling. She's weird. In conversations, I think I mostly look at the other person's mouth. But when she talks to me, she looks right in my eyes . . . and barely ever blinks.

"You and Georgie almost crushed me into the wall. So. Anyway. Here's the deal. If you get Georgie to invite me to his pizza party, I'll invite both of you to mine."

"Umm, I don't know. It's up to him," I said. She has straight teeth. I am going to have to wear braces starting next year.

"I have a small appetite. So it would be a good trade. Because, you know, Georgie eats a lot."

Of course Georgie would say yes.

"I'll try," I mumbled.

She continued smiling and staring. Her hair is black and very shiny.

I know what you're thinking, but Lana is *not* my girlfriend, and since I'm the one who is writing this

book, and I know what happened, I can promise that there are no girlfriends in this book.

Lana then asked me to call her house and tell her Georgie's answer. I don't even know her telephone number, and before I could tell her to call Georgie herself, Mrs. Crespo walked up, congratulated Lana on winning one of the prizes, and turned to me.

"I am not quite certain what to do about your sister's actions today, Ronald. I think that I shall leave it up to you."

Mrs. Crespo seemed to be waiting for me to say

something, but since Lana was there, I didn't speak. It's not that what I would decide to do about Goon would be secret or anything. It's just that Lana was staring at me, and that made me nervous. Not nervous exactly, maybe more like shy.

"It's your choice, Ronald. You may explain the situation to your parents or not," Mrs. Crespo went on. "If they wish, they may telephone me."

Mrs. Crespo said good-bye and walked away, leaving me standing there with still-staring-at-me Lana Shen and Rachel Campos, a classmate who had just sort of appeared next to Lana while I wasn't looking. Rachel whispered to Lana. Lana giggled and waved, then they ran to get their backpacks and headed out the playground gate.

I looked around. Only Georgie and I were left. The school was deserted. Fifth grade was finished.

We had the rest of June. Then July and August. But no camp in Maine.

Summer.

Bummer.

Chapter 12

A Face in the Window . . . and the Evidence

As we rode away from school, I was thinking about what Mrs. Crespo had said. I was also thinking about the Point Battle. Goon would be in big trouble if I tattled. And big trouble for Goon meant big points for me.

Here's how I figured it. (If you forgot how the Point Battle works, please look back at Chapter 6.)

1. School punishment equals 8 points; punishment by Mom or Dad, only 4. This one was tricky. Since the incident occurred at school, but the punishment would come from Mom and Dad, I thought that 6 points would be a fair compromise.

2. Since I was the one who exposed her crime, double it to 12 points.
3. Since it would undoubtedly be a big punishment, double it again to 24 points.
4. Since Goon lied and was caught, double it again to 48 points.

There has never been a 48-point win in the history of the Point Battle. With Goon currently ahead 623–592, this would put me in the lead, 640–623! The last time I was ahead, I was in fourth grade and the score was only 17–15!

"You want to stop and see if there's a reply?" Georgie asked.

"Huh?" I had been pedaling and thinking and had no idea what he was talking about.

"The Toad, remember?"

We were just turning the corner onto Eureka Avenue. I nodded and accelerated, passing Georgie and zooming down the street toward the old green-gray house. I skidded to a stop, almost knocking over the recycling can again. I heard my mind saying, *Whew! That would've been hard to explain.* Then

I peered over the fence that guarded the front yard.

"See anything?" Georgie asked as he stopped his bike next to mine.

"Nope. Hold my bike." Remembering my disastrous exit through the bushes last time, I went around to the front gate, opened it, and walked along the flat rocks that led up to the front steps. I had not forgotten that Officer Crompton had told us to stay away from The Haunted Toad, but because our note was gone, I figured that G. J. Prott had sort of invited us to trespass so that we could see if there was a reply.

(Now that I'm writing this, I'm not sure my reasoning was logical, but that's what I was thinking back then.)

I climbed the steps and looked around. Nothing. I turned toward Georgie and shook my head.

"What's that under the mat?" he whispered very loudly.

A white corner peeked out. I reached down, lifted the mat, and there, next to a bunch of sow bugs, was a small white envelope.

I know you want to know what was in the envelope,

and for sure that's more important than sow bugs, but sow bugs are my favorite insects, mainly because they are *not* insects. I have included two drawings, so just in case you don't know what a sow bug is, you'll know what non-insect I'm talking about.

A sow bug is also called a roly-poly or a pill bug, depending on where you live. (If you use a different name, please go to my website and tell me. I have a whole page about sow bugs.) They don't have wings. They are brownish or gray and have seven pairs of legs. They also have tiny overlapping armor plates that make them look like little armadillos. I like that. And they roll up into little balls when disturbed. I like that, too. But here's what's so cool. These non-insects are actually crustaceans and are close relatives of shrimp and lobsters.

Okay, I love to eat shrimp, and I *really* love lobster.

Gloucester is famous for lobster. We have tons of lobster fishermen who go out in their boats and set lots of lobster traps—they call them pots—in the Atlantic Ocean. You can buy lobsters right down at the harbor.

So here's the question I have not had the courage to answer. If someone cooked and ate a sow bug, would it taste like shrimp or lobster? Or would it be disgustingly gross? I am *not* going to try it, and the people who published this book don't want you to try it, either. So . . . DON'T TRY IT! AND DON'T EMAIL ME!

I walked back to my bike holding up the small envelope for Georgie to see.

"Let's get out of sight before we open it," Georgie said.

I shook my head. "Nope. Let's open it here. Maybe G. J. Prott has been waiting for us to come back and is watching us right now from one of the windows."

Both of us looked back at the house, our eyes moving from window to window, but we saw nothing unusual. I tore open the envelope. Here's what was inside:

Messrs. Sinkoff and Mack:
I am interested in what was in the old envelope
you found. Please come to my home at 9:00 in
the morning tomorrow.
                          Yours truly,
                          G. J. Prott

"What's M-E-S-S-R-S?" I asked as I stuck the letter
back in the envelope.

"Maybe ol' Prott saw us mess up that next-door
lady's trash and thinks we're messers, and he or she
or it can't spell," Georgie replied.

That seemed like a really good answer, but I actually looked up "Messrs." It is the plural of Mr., and
it's pronounced exactly like "messers." Weird.

"Tomorrow morning two mysteries will be solved.
Who is G. J. Prott? And"—I did my spookiest "ow-
hooo-eeeee" and grinned devilishly—"what creepy
creeps creep around inside The Haunted Toad?"

But Georgie wasn't paying attention. His mouth
was open, and he was staring straight at The Haunted
Toad. I followed his eyes. There, on the third floor, the

curtains were parted, and a very small, very old woman stared back at us.

Georgie and I moved away from The Haunted Toad, walking our bikes, looking over our shoulders, never taking our eyes off the face in the window. The woman didn't wave, didn't smile, didn't even move. When we couldn't see the window any longer, I touched Georgie's arm, and he jumped.

"This is turning out to be the strangest day of my entire life," I said softly. We got on our bikes and pedaled slowly.

We had only ridden one block when Georgie surprised me by stopping and asking, "Let me see the penny."

I took it out of my backpack and handed it to him. He looked at it carefully, turning it over a few times in the sunlight.

"This does not look like it's over a hundred years old. It's barely worn."

"So?"

"I don't know. But if we return this penny and the necklace, what if Prott says thanks and that's all?"

Georgie did his disappearing coin trick. "Then we've got nothing. I found it. It was in my house. Finders keepers."

"Come on, Georgie. We left a note. That's kind of like a promise."

"Then we'll just return the necklace."

"We might get a reward, remember?" I said.

"Maybe. But I bet we'll get the same crummy reward for returning the necklace all by itself."

"The penny's only worth three bucks."

"You said the value depended on its condition. Maybe you don't know how to tell." He put the coin in his pants pocket and started riding. "Follow me."

We coasted down the hill toward the Inner Harbor. At first I couldn't guess where he was going. But when we got down to Main Street, I knew. There was a coin and stamp store close to the pet store where he had gotten the mice. It was in between a bakery and a shoe repair.

We leaned our bikes against a squat statue of an old cobbler holding up a shoe and went into the coin shop. The door had a bell hooked to it that jingled loudly and kept jingling for a long time. The store's glass cases were filled with stamps, coins, old paper money, and lots of old medals, some of them with fancy ribbons. There was no one in the store.

"Hello?" Georgie said.

We heard a toilet flush, and a moment later a very skinny man came out from the back.

"May I help you?"

"Yeah," Georgie said. "We have this penny, and we'd like to know what it's worth."

"Do you want to sell it?"

"Maybe," I said.

Georgie took the penny out of his pocket and put it on the counter. The man took a small brown envelope from a drawer.

"Whose name should I put on this?"

"We just want to know what you'd pay us for it," Georgie said.

"I understand. I'm the bookkeeper. Mr. Whelan won't be back until this evening. If you leave the coin for appraisal, he'll look at it tonight, and you can come back tomorrow morning to pick it up or sell it."

Georgie gave the man his name and got a receipt.

We didn't talk on the way home, so I guess Georgie thought I was upset with him. I really wasn't. Or maybe I was. I could sort of see his point. But I also . . . I don't know. I wasn't sure what was right.

A couple of blocks from our houses, where our streets diverged (good word . . . it means going in different directions), I called out, "See you after dinner." We had planned that he would sleep over. Georgie waved, then disappeared around the corner.

I'd been thinking about Georgie and the penny and The Haunted Toad so much that I'd completely forgotten about Goon and the ticket stubs. But as I rode my bike up our driveway, there she was, sitting on our front porch. She was eating celery and dip and staring right at me. I thought about what she'd done at my party. Mrs. Crespo had said I could decide. Should I tattle on her or not?

Because everything I have written so far about my sister makes her seem rotten, you might think that she is completely rotten. That is not true. Goon has many excellent qualities. Here is my list:

1. She bathes frequently.

2. She doesn't step on insects.

3. Because of her many years of ballet, she
   can balance on one foot until everyone
   watching her is bored.

4. I can't think of any others right now,
   but if I do, I will come back and put them
   in, so if you are reading this, you know I
   couldn't come up with any more.

"Want some bean dip?" Goon asked.

I was suspicious. Why was she acting nice? I leaned my bike against the porch and took the celery stalk she offered. I scooped up some of the dip, but didn't eat. Maybe she had poisoned the stuff. But after she stuck her celery in and took a bite of dip, chewed, and swallowed, I bit off the end of mine.

She instantly laughed. "I spit in the dip, stupid runt!"

I sort of coughed, then spit the half-chewed hunk out, hitting Goon in the neck and cheek with threads of celery covered in bean dip. She jumped up and pushed me off the first step. I'm not grossed out by

Spit dip!

spit—it's not poison or anything like that—but puking it back at her seemed like the right thing to do.

"You just blew it!" I shouted. "I wasn't going to tell Mom and Dad about how you hid my tickets. Mrs. Crespo left it up to me, and I wasn't. But now——"

She came after me, but I ran. I am faster than she is by far. I was all the way to the sidewalk before she had gone eight steps.

"You can't prove I did anything!" she yelled, stopping in the middle of the yard.

"I'll give you one chance," I taunted, bouncing from foot to foot. "You actually did me and Georgie a favor. Because of your cheating, you guaranteed that we would win, so I'll forget the whole thing if you apologize."

"I am going to totally kill you."

"That does not sound like an apology."

She charged, but just before she reached me, I faked her out by taking a step toward the driveway, then ducking around her and running up the front steps. That's one of my best moves in touch football. I was inside the house and down the hall before she even reached the front door.

At times like this, I always prefer Mom to be the judge. She is very smart and really hard to trick. Dad is also very smart, but I think he is more of a softy. Sometimes he is just too willing to believe Goon, even when he should know she is lying. Granpa doesn't like to get involved in kid arguments. "I get enough of that crap-eroo all summer long," he always says.

My running and Goon's chasing were not exactly quiet, so when I charged into Dad's office, he knew trouble had arrived.

"Stop," he commanded. "Stand right here." He pointed at the side of his desk. Goon hurtled in a moment later, ready to clobber me.

"What's going on?" Dad asked.

"I wasn't going to say anything about what Junie did at my party," I started, "but—"

(Notice that I do not call her Goon in front of my parents. You can probably guess why.)

Goon interrupted. "I'm not going to stand around and listen to him lie." She turned to leave like she had done with Mrs. Crespo, but Dad called her name in a stern voice, and she froze.

It took an eternity for me to tell Dad about the ticket stubs because Goon kept interrupting with "Liar!" and "It's his word against mine!" and "He has no proof!"

Dad just listened, and when he had heard enough, he put up his hand . . . and the room got quiet.

"Junie," he said, "give me your shorts."

I was surprised, but Goon was so stunned, her mouth hung open.

Finally she shook her head. "No."

Dad started to stand, which would have meant huge trouble, so Goon gave in instantly. She unbuttoned her shorts, dropped them around her ankles, and stepped out. She looked *really* angry.

I know some families are modest—Dad calls it "uptight"—about underwear, but our family is pretty relaxed, at least about me and Goon. Mom demands certain "standards of decency." For example, we are not allowed to come to the dinner table in underwear, and Granpa is not allowed to watch the Red Sox in his boxer shorts, which bothers him because he claims to have a lucky pair he won off Big Papi in a poker game—which I think is a total lie. Granpa says if you don't know who Big Papi is and you like baseball, you should "hang your head, move to New York, and become a stinking Yankee fan." IMO, he takes watching the Red Sox way too seriously.

Dad stuck out his hand, and Goon kicked her shorts over to him. He picked them up and peered into her back pockets for a long time. Finally he looked up at me.

"What color were your tickets, Ronald?"

"Red. Bright red."

Dad nodded, then leaned back in his chair and spoke to Goon in a very friendly voice, which, because of what he said, sounded ominous. (I just learned that word. It means—ow-hooo-eeeee—something spooky bad is going to happen.)

"Based on the evidence, I know exactly what occurred. So I'm going to give you a chance to tell the truth. Listen up, Junie. Small penalty for the truth. Big penalty for a lie."

"What evidence?" Goon asked. She did not sound so cocky.

"I'm the one asking the questions here," Dad answered quickly.

Goon fidgeted, sort of rocking from one foot to the other. I did a quick calculation in my head. If Goon told the truth and Dad gave her a "small penalty" like he said, I'd get only 24 points because there'd be no doubling for "big punishment." With the current score 623–592, 24 points would only bump it up to 623–616, and I'd still be behind. This was my big chance. I needed her to lie, so I began chanting to myself, "Lie, lie, lie."

I guess my lips must have been moving because Goon looked at me and said, "Shut up."

"Time's up," Dad said. "What's the story?"

Goon stood there like a statue. She looked angry or frightened or ready to cry . . . I couldn't tell which. She had to answer Dad, but would it be the truth or a lie?

Before you read any further, guess what she did. The answer is in the next chapter. But don't peek!

Chapter 13
A Silhouette in the Dark

Did you make a guess? Well, I did, too. While Goon was squirming, here's how I thought about it:

1. I was sure that Goon had put the stubs in her back pocket at the beginning of the party. I saw her do it.

2. I was certain that she would have thrown them away before she got home. (My sister is mean, but also very smart. She gets excellent grades in middle school and is especially good in science. Last year she built a model volcano that erupted out fake lava and smoke and really stunk up the science fair. Very cool.)

3. I could not guess what evidence Dad had

found. Maybe there was none and he was trying to trick her into confessing.

4. I was sure that Goon was thinking the same thing, so it seemed likely that she would continue to lie.

5. But maybe Goon would tell the truth because she knew that Dad hates lying more than anything. If he caught her lying, she'd get some gargantuan (you should learn this word—it means humungous but is *much* classier) removal of privileges, like maybe not getting to go to Camp Leeward. That would be awful for Goon and also *terrible* for me. It's bad enough having to miss camp in order to be with Georgie, but for Goon to stay home, too? Ugh! Or maybe Dad would let her go to camp, but make sure that instead of having fun with her friends she would have to sort the mail or do other camp chores for Lois. (Remember Lois? I mentioned her many chapters ago, so

maybe you forgot that she's Granpa's ex-wife, and she owns the camps.)

After thinking about all this, I decided she would lie.

What did you decide?

* * *

Answer: Truth. Goon confessed.

Her punishment? Not much. Just two weeks of doing my dishwashing duty, a puny penalty. And Dad actually thanked her for not lying. I only got 24 points. I'm still behind in the Point Battle.

Later I asked Dad about the evidence, but he said, "Case closed."

It's a mystery. If you have a good idea of what Dad knew, please go to the evidence page on my website.

After dinner, Georgie came over with his father. Mr. Sinkoff had bought us a super-giant, super-gooey éclair for dessert. Yum. When he went into the den to talk with my dad, we ran into the kitchen and divided the éclair. Very messy!

I had just picked up my half when Goon walked

in, heading for the refrigerator. She elbowed me "accidentally" as she passed, smooshing my nose into the éclair filling.

I would not even mention this except for the Point Battle. Gunking up my nose with Georgie watching would be worth 2 points for Goon. That's why I waited while she grabbed some grapes from the fridge. When she turned around, I slowly wiped the goo off my nose, licked my finger, and said, "Oh my gosh! This is the most delicious treat I have ever had in my whole life. Too bad there's only enough for two kids."

She couldn't do anything except stick out her tongue. What a baby! Insult canceled. No points for her.

Meanwhile, Dad and Mr. Sinkoff were setting up stuff in the den for their monthly poker game. I think there are eight men who play, but they do it at a different house each time, so they're only at my house one and a half times each year.

(Okay. I know that it's impossible to be at my house *a half of a time*. But twelve months divided by eight men does equal 1.5, so . . . Aha! I just called Glenn

Philips. He said I am right, but there's a better way to say it: *They're only at my house three times every two years.* If you don't understand, Glenn's explanation is on my website. You can look at it there.)

By the time we finished our éclairs (I had to wash my face!), a couple of my dad's friends had arrived, so we went upstairs to my room. I flipped the light switch, which turned on the lamp on my bedside table. Deeb was lying in the middle of the room. Georgie took two steps in, spun halfway around, and did a huge back-flop onto the bed. Deeb jumped up beside him. Georgie held his nose and pushed her off. I sat in my desk chair and called to her. She settled down next to me.

No one said anything for a while. Finally Georgie gave out a big sigh and said, "Cheesie, when we go to The Toad tomorrow . . ." And then he stopped and pulled a pillow over his head.

"You afraid?"

"Of what? A little old lady? Heck no!"

He threw the pillow at me, but I batted it down. There was another long silence while I booted up my computer and Georgie tossed the tennis ball that I keep next to my bed up toward the ceiling.

(Sometimes when I'm reading in bed, I squeeze that tennis ball over and over. I have developed a very strong grip for someone my size. You should try it.)

The movement of the ball got Deeb's attention. She lifted her head and followed it with her eyes, but her body never moved.

"Georgie, we should give the penny back," I said. "What if there's, like, a curse on it?"

"A curse (toss)? Get serious (toss)."

"That would explain the invisible writing."

"There was no invisible writing (toss)."

"Sort of was. Eureka, remember?"

"Cheesie, listen (toss). The note we left didn't say *what* was in the envelope (toss). It just said there was *something* (toss). The necklace is enough. Ol' Prott will be thrilled." Georgie put the ball down and pulled the coin store receipt out of his pocket and read aloud, "'Lincoln Head cent—1909-S.' I really want to keep it. It's the coolest thing I ever found in my whole life." He dropped the receipt on the bed.

Goon must have been lurking and spying in the hallway because she suddenly zipped into my room and snatched up the receipt. "What's this?"

"None of your beeswax!" I said, grabbing for it. The receipt ripped, leaving me with just a scrap showing the coin store's name and address. "Give it back!" I shouted, but she ran across the hall into her room and locked the door.

(Granpa taught me to say "none of your beeswax." He says it's what kids used to say when he was a boy.)

I banged on her door. "Gimme that piece of paper! If Dad comes up here . . . If I tell him . . . You're gonna be in big trouble again."

The door opened suddenly. "I hid it." She grinned. "Tell me everything, or else you'll never find it."

"There's nothing to tell," I said. "It's a penny. That's all." Georgie stood right behind me nodding his head.

"Don't fib me, runt. I read what's on that paper. It's really old. Where'd you get it? You stole that coin, didn't you?"

"Shut up. Georgie found it in his basement. It's no

big deal. It's only worth three bucks. I'll prove it." I spun around and went back into my room, plopped down in my desk chair, and pulled up the website that showed how much old Lincoln cents were worth. I started to point. I started to speak.

But I was speechless.

Remember about a million pages back how I said I had made a mistake by looking up the 1909 coin instead of the 1909-S? It was right at this moment that I saw my error.

"What?" Goon demanded.

I'm sure Georgie didn't know why I wasn't answering, but he jumped in anyway, pointing at the monitor. "See. 1909. Three bucks. Give me my receipt."

Goon looked at the screen, made a face, and pulled the torn receipt out of her pocket. (Some hiding place!) She crumpled it into a wad, threw it at my head, and left, slamming the door behind her.

Georgie retrieved the wadded receipt, took the other half out of my hand, pieced them together, and put them on the desk. He sat back on my bed and began tossing the tennis ball again. "Your sister is a jerk." Then he noticed my weird expression. "What?"

"The penny is worth more than three bucks."

Still tossing the tennis ball, Georgie asked, "What do you mean?"

"I forgot the San Francisco thing when I looked before. The mint mark. The S. Omigosh, Georgie. You're not going to believe this. It's worth ninety-five dollars!"

"What?!" Georgie flubbed his catch and knocked over my bedside lamp. The room went dark except for the eerie light from my computer screen.

One second later there was a knock on the door.

I yelled, "Go away, Goon!" Then the knock repeated, and so did I. "Go away!" We sat in the dark for a few seconds, then the door slowly opened. Silhouetted in the doorway stood a man I did not recognize. (I am not making this up!) It was like in the movies where the crazy guy with the chain saw comes in to murder the dim-witted teenagers who stay in the old farmhouse way longer than any intelligent people would have.

Then the man stepped forward, and the light from my computer lit one side of his face. It was Officer Crompton.

My brain went completely blackout for a second and then started thinking at super speed:

1. Since Officer Crompton was not in his uniform, he was doing some kind of undercover mystery investigation.

2. Since he was at my house, the mystery involved my family.

3. Since he was in my room, and Georgie and I had been sort of arrested by him earlier today, he was investigating us.

4. Since the only thing we had done that might be mysterious was to mention in the note we gave to the old lady that there was something in the envelope we found, she must have called the police.

5. Therefore, Officer Crompton was here to find out what was in the envelope.

"Hello, boys. Remember me?"

I nodded. Georgie also nodded, but he was in deeper

shadow than I was, so Officer Crompton probably couldn't tell.

"I'm guessing you don't know why I'm here."

We both shook our heads. But we were not thinking the same thing. I was pretty sure that Georgie's head shake was agreeing that he *didn't* know. My head shake was *dis*agreeing because I was pretty sure I did.

Without thinking, I reached toward my backpack. In the light that came in from the hall and from my computer, I could clearly see the old yellowed envelope sticking out of one of the pockets. Then I realized that a policeman on an investigation would probably be watching me for suspicious movements, so I kept moving my arm until I was petting Deeb. Then I looked back at Officer Crompton.

"I know you told us to stay away from The Toad— I mean, G. J. Prott's house," I said. "But tomorrow, we—I mean, the envelope and stuff was lost in Georgie's house for over fifty years and even though, as Georgie says, finders keepers, we're going to—"

Officer Crompton put up his hand, so I stopped talking.

"I was on duty this afternoon. Now I'm here playing cards with my friends." He gave a sly grin. "And to remind you two to keep out of trouble." He tossed off a sloppy salute—Dad showed me the Navy way years ago—and walked down the hall, leaving my bedroom door open.

Neither Georgie nor I said a word until we heard Officer Crompton going down the stairs.

"Glenn Philips was right," I said, turning on my desk lamp. "Officer Crompton doesn't know every kid in town by sight. He knew who we were today because he's been to our houses before. I guess I just never noticed who my dad's pals—"

Does NOT know every kid in Gloucester . . . whew! ⟶

"Whatever," Georgie said. "And come on, why'd you blab all that about the envelope?"

I did not have a good answer. "I dunno. I guess I just talk stupid when the police are around."

"Well, it doesn't matter because tomorrow we're going to sell that penny and get ninety-five dollars. Our summer may not be completely ruined. That's

170

enough to go to Six Flags. There's some cool new rides that're absolutely guaranteed to make you barf!"

"I don't know. I think Officer Crompton will be watching—"

"Forget Crompton!"

We sat there in the semidark for a while. Finally I said, "It would be fun to go on the new rides."

Then Georgie reminded me about the last time we went to the amusement park. We talked for a long time, and then, with Deeb dog-snoring at the foot of my bed, we fell asleep laughing about our sno-cone fight and our backward dizzy walk challenge.

(I don't think I need to describe these. You can probably guess.)

Chapter 14
Entering The Haunted Toad

I woke up early and just lay there thinking about roller coasters. Georgie was asleep on his back, one

arm flopped completely out of the covers. I was in such a good mood that I decided to play a practical joke on him, one that my dad once told me he'd done to his cousin when they were kids.

I got a can of shaving cream from Granpa's bathroom and squirted a huge glob onto the palm of Georgie's outstretched

hand. Then I took the feather out of a Robin Hood hat I've had for a million years and gently, very gently,

 tickled Georgie's nose. He twitched. I tickled it again. He squirmed. I tick-led it once more, and his hand swung up to shoo away the fly that he was probably dreaming about. Sploosh! A face full of shaving cream!

If you decide to try this practical joke on someone bigger than you— like Georgie is to me—be prepared to run.

Georgie woke up, realized what had happened, and attacked. But I was ready. I ran to the bathroom and

locked the door. Georgie pounded, and our noise woke up the rest of the house and gave Goon a reason to be crabby all morning.

After I fed Deeb (on my hands and knees, remem-ber?), Georgie and I celebrated our secret plan to sell the penny and go to Six Flags by eating a gargantuan number of gobbler wraps. Everyone else calls them pigs in a blanket—breakfast sausages rolled up in pancakes—but Dad likes turkey sausage instead of pork, so he came up with a new name. Goon ate only pancakes. Because she is a vegetarian, she calls sausages "flesh tubes." It doesn't bother me one bit.

We were in such a good mood that we forgot about the time. Suddenly I jumped up and grabbed my backpack. "Come on, Georgie! We're late."

"Where're you going?" Mom asked.

"Out." When she gave me another raised eyebrow, I added, "Georgie and I volunteered to help some lady."

I shouldn't have offered so much information. Mom pressed. "Who is she? And where does she live?"

"We don't know her name. She's really old. We found an envelope she lost, and we're returning it, and she lives about halfway to school. We'll be back before lunch." I was out the door before Mom could ask any more questions.

"You lied to your mother," Georgie said as we got on our bikes.

"Did not."

"You said you didn't know the old lady's name."

"I don't. *Someone* signed the note 'G. J. Prott.' But maybe it wasn't the lady in the window. Could've been her second husband's sister's stepson. Who knows?" I stood up on my pedals and yelled, "Beat you to The Toad!" The race was on!

We had only gone two blocks, with me ahead as usual, when Georgie yelled, "The coin store!" and made a U-turn.

I braked, skidded to a stop, and turned around, but Georgie was way ahead. I had no chance to catch up. He was straddling his bike and leaning against the cobbler statue when I got to the stamp and coin dealer's store.

"It's closed."

I looked at the sign on the front door—"Open at 10 a.m."—and then at the clock on the wall inside. It was 8:50.

"This actually helps," I told Georgie. "We'll go to The Toad and give back the envelope and the necklace. And we don't have to lie about the penny. We'll mention it, but since we don't actually have it, maybe . . ." I paused to think. "Let me do the talking."

Now that I had actually seen that someone lived in The Haunted Toad, the house seemed very different to me. Before, it was the building itself that was alive. Georgie and I had pretended that it breathed, had thoughts, and maybe even moved when we weren't looking. Now the structure was just wood and windows, green-gray and still. But the insides had changed entirely. The ghosts that we knew weren't real had become an old woman who we knew was.

We leaned our bikes against the front fence and went through the gate.

"I admit it," Georgie said. "This is very spooky."

"Me too. What if the old lady has a crazy nephew locked in the attic? Or if she turned all her dead relatives into mummies and they're sitting in chairs all around the house? Or if she has a room filled with tarantu—?"

"Cool it, Cheesie. This isn't funny."

We walked up the porch stairs. They creaked loudly, and I thought how Granpa would have been impressed with how I avoided the squeaks the last time. There was no doorbell. Just an enormous metal knocker shaped like an artichoke.

Georgie reached for the knocker.

"Remember, let me do the talking," I cautioned.

"Sure. You did so well with the policeman. Blither, blather, blah, blah, blah." He grinned at me, then got serious. "Here goes." He lifted the artichoky thing and let go. The knocker fell, but stopped itself before hitting the door. No sound. Georgie tried it again. Nothing. Georgie looked at me with a what-do-I-do-now face. This would have been an excellent time for me to do my "ow-hooo-eeeee" wail, but to be honest, I was a little bit anxious myself. I pushed by him, lifted the knocker, and yanked it down hard. It hit the metal plate with an enormous clank, then pulled completely off the door and almost smashed my foot.

I picked it up and was trying to hook it back on when the door opened. The old woman stood in the doorway. She was tiny, smaller even than Mrs. Crespo. Her hair was pure white and bunched up inside a cloth hat that was the same green-gray color as The Toad.

Her eyes, also the same color, flicked back and forth between me and Georgie, and her hands fluttered like small wings.

"Am I mistaken? Or are you Messrs. Sinkoff and Mack?" She spoke very rapidly. Her words were like sweet, sharp notes on a piccolo.

(It took me a long time to write that last sentence because it was really hard to find the right description. She had the most unusual voice I have ever heard.)

"I'm Ronald Mack," I said. "And he's Georgie Sinkoff."

"Please come in. Of course, I've been expecting you, and you are right on time. Excellent. Excellent. Come in." Everything about her from the waist up was in constant motion. She waved her arms to indicate that we should step inside. Her head nodded repeatedly to show us that if we did, we'd be doing the right thing. Her mouth smiled, then didn't, and repeated that over and over. She blinked a lot.

I set the metal artichoke down on the porch, and we went in.

Inside, The Toad was dark and cool. It smelled sugary and musty. It wasn't unpleasant. It was sort of like when my dad turns the car heater on after we haven't used it for a long time.

She closed the door, and the normal sounds of town totally disappeared. I couldn't hear any cars or birds or wind or airplanes. It was as if The Toad was a soundproof chamber deep inside a mountain or something. The place was stuffed with old furniture and other old junk. It looked to me like she hadn't bought anything new in a long time.

"Please sit in there." She pointed into a room. "Yes. There are chairs, a sofa—two sofas, actually. Choose whatever suits you."

Even though her motions and speech were rapid, her progress from the front door to the parlor was unbelievably slow. (She didn't call it a parlor. I just thought it looked way too old-fashioned to be called a living room.) Hands fluttering, she walked with extremely small, very careful steps, like she was a tightrope walker balanced way above the ground.

Georgie sat carefully on one of the sofas. I scooted

in next to him. The cushion was very fat and felt like no one had ever sat on it.

The woman finally got to a small chair. It took her a long time to change from standing to sitting, but when she did, everything slow and frail about her disappeared.

"I should introduce myself," she said. "Yes. That's the proper thing to do. You have introduced yourselves, and I should do the same. My name is Glenora Jean Prott. I'm ninety-six years old. That must seem remarkably old to you. It surely does to me. Who would ever, when she was a girl your age—I'm guessing you boys are eleven or twelve. Or maybe you—your name is Georgie?— you might be thirteen. Am I right? Am I wrong?"

I started to speak, but didn't.

"Who would ever guess one would live so long? I surely didn't. But then, no one really thinks about such things when just a young girl, does one?"

I shook my head. Georgie did, too. Georgie's eyes were wide, and his mouth was hanging open in a way that did not make him look very intelligent. I bet I looked stupid, too.

Glenora Jean Prott plucked a piece of paper out of a pocket of her sweater. It was the note we had left her.

"So, young gentlemen. You found an envelope. An envelope you think was once mailed to me." Her smile was like a lightbulb: on, off, on, off.

I took off my backpack and swung it around onto my lap, hitting Georgie in the head in the process. He was in a trance or something. He didn't even flinch.

"We did. I mean Georgie did. It was in his basement." I took out the envelope. "Did you used to live at thirty-nine Sutcliffe Street?"

"Oh, yes. For many years." She nodded several times. I guess she was emphasizing how long it was. "I was born in Pennsylvania, but I lived in Nova Scotia as a young girl. That's Canada. But you must know that. Am I right? Am I wrong?" She tilted her head several times.

I thought she might be waiting for an answer, so I said, "You're right." I knew where Nova Scotia was. It's a province. That's like a state.

"My father was a mining engineer. Coal mining. He

took me into a coal mine once. You cannot imagine how dark it is in a coal mine. Well, actually, I suspect you can imagine how dark it is. Sutcliffe Street . . ." She paused and moved one finger in the palm of her other hand, like she was counting the years. "We moved there when I was eighteen. And we moved here after my father passed away. 1957. Late in the year." She paused and looked up at the ceiling. "He died in autumn."

While she was talking, I had taken the old envelope out of my backpack and emptied the heart necklace into my hand. I reached over and handed her the envelope. She smiled, then peered at it closely.

"Oh, my!" Her hands flew up to her face, sort of crushing the envelope against her cheek. "This is my sister's handwriting." She began to cry.

Not counting TV and movies and Aunt Brenda's wedding when I was six—Meemo was bawling because she was so happy that her youngest daughter finally got married—I had never seen a grown-up cry. So when Glenora Jean Prott cried, I had no idea how to react. I just sat absolutely still. I was right next to

Georgie, but I couldn't even turn my head to look at him. After a few moments, Georgie poked me with a box of tissues that had been sitting on the lamp table next to him. I took the box, and when I gave it to her, I realized that I was still holding the heart necklace.

"Oh, and this"—I held out the necklace—"was in the envelope and there was a . . ." Her eyes widened, and then she sobbed, and maybe she didn't hear me say, ". . . penny in there, too."

Her hand, which had amazed me by moving so fast when she spoke, now moved very slowly toward the necklace, finally touching the heart.

"Elaine's . . . ," she said, wiping her eyes with a tissue. "It was Elaine's. She sent it to me when she knew she was . . ." Glenora Jean Prott took a deep breath and stopped crying. "When she knew she was dying." She took the necklace, cupped her hands around the heart like a hug, and smiled. "I lost it when we moved here to Eureka Avenue. Oh, I was so miserably sad about it." She looked up at us. "Where did you boys find it?"

"It was in Georgie's basement . . . where you used to live," I said. "Stuck behind some wood under the stairs. Right, Georgie?"

He nodded.

She dabbed her eyes with a tissue. "I had torn the corner off the envelope so I could write Elaine's new address in my address book. And then the envelope was gone. I must have dropped it down the cellar stairs. Oh, you cannot imagine how unhappy I was." She looked at Georgie. "Was it you who found it?"

Georgie nodded.

Her on-off-on-off smile came back. It made me feel good to see her smile.

"Did you know that this opens up?" she asked, holding up the silver heart.

Georgie shook his head and looked at me. I shook my head, too.

"Come look, boys."

We wiggled off the puffy couch and came closer. Georgie stayed sort of hunched over behind me, like he was using me as a shield. Glenora Jean Prott held up the heart and used a fingernail to press a hidden niche that neither Georgie nor I had noticed. It popped open like a clamshell. Inside were two pictures of grown women, one on each side.

"This is Elaine," Glenora Jean Prott said, pointing at one of the tiny photos. Georgie leaned over me to see better. "She was the beautiful and smart Prott sister. She was only forty-eight when she died. It was the cancer, you know."

"Is this other lady you?" I asked.

Glenora Jean Prott nodded several times. I could tell that she had almost completely

recovered from her sadness—except her eyes were still reddish—because her head and hands and eyes and everything were moving full-speed again. And I suddenly figured out that she was Ms. Prott, not Mrs. Prott.

Can you guess how I knew? The answer is at the end of this chapter.

Georgie leaned even closer and peered at Ms. Prott's tiny photo. "I think this woman—I mean you—was very pretty." It was such a surprising thing for Georgie to say, especially because he hadn't said one word since coming into the house.

Ms. Prott beamed and touched Georgie on the head. There was a long silence. I was pretty sure she was thinking about her sister. Then she stood up and began to walk slowly out of the room. When she got to the door, she said, "Please wait." She went around the corner, and we heard her small steps.

"What are we going to do about the penny?" Georgie whispered.

I shrugged. "I don't know."

I heard the small steps returning.

She reentered the room carrying a framed picture. She came toward us and turned it around so we could look at it. It was a photograph of two young women, all dressed up, doing a very crazy dance.

"This is Elaine." She pointed at one of the two women, and then nodded her head several times and smiled on-off-on-off. "This is me. Actually, I was a better dancer." She giggled. I had never heard an old woman giggle. It made me smile.

"Umm, we also found a penny in the envelope." The words just popped out of my mouth. "But we didn't bring it." I looked at Georgie. He was expressionless.

"A 1909 penny . . ." Her voice trailed off sort of like she wasn't even aware that she had spoken out loud.

"Uh-huh," I said softly. The penny must have been really special to her if she remembered the date after all these years. Finders keepers, Georgie had said, but now it looked like we would give it back. That would mean no money for Six Flags. I had the torn-up receipt from the coin store in my backpack. We'd just go pick the penny up and bring it to Ms. Prott's house. (I'm not going to call it The Haunted Toad anymore.)

"Elaine was born in 1909. She was older than me. Yes. She was quite an athlete, too. Oh my, yes. She excelled in tennis and could run faster than almost anyone. When she learned she was dying, she sent me that penny." She leaned back in her chair and hugged the photograph to her chest. "She sent me that penny, that very special penny, because she wanted me to have something that was exactly as old as she was . . . something that would never die."

Georgie made a little sound in his throat. I glanced at him. His eyes were watery. Maybe mine were, too.

* * *

Ms. or Mrs. Prott?

1. She told us that she and Elaine were the Prott sisters.
2. That meant that they both had the same last name.
3. In the olden days women always changed their last name when they got married.
4. Glenora Jean was still a Prott, so she didn't change her name.

5. Therefore, she never got married and was
   Ms. Prott.

I checked this logic with Glenn Philips, and he said I was probably correct. If you think I am wrong or that there is another possibility, please go to my website and tell me your idea.

Chapter 15
How Much Is One Cent Worth?

I looked over at Georgie. "We'll go get the penny and bring it back."

"We'll bring the penny back to you," Georgie echoed.

Ms. Prott thanked us and walked us out, but because of her slowness and our fastness, we were already on our bikes by the time she waved to us from the front door. She was still holding the photograph of the two dancing sisters.

"I always get a little dizzy on roller coasters anyway!" I shouted to Georgie as we biked back toward the coin store.

"Me too!"

Two liars. That's what we were. I absolutely *never*

get dizzy on roller coasters, and Georgie is way braver than I am. I bet there isn't a roller coaster anywhere that Georgie wouldn't try.

Our summer kept changing. We were going to camp . . . and then not. We were going to Six Flags . . . and then not. Granpa says that if you ever think you know what life is going to bring you next, stay alert because that's when you're going to be surprised.

And if right now you're reading this and you think you know what happened to me and Georgie next . . . well, get ready to be surprised.

The coin shop was still closed when we arrived. The clock inside said 9:40. We had a twenty-minute wait. We rocked back and forth on our bikes. Then we got hit with a terrific smell from the bakery next door.

Georgie said, "Man, I'm hungry."

Remember the five-dollar bill from Gumpy I'd stashed in my backpack? Georgie and I leaned our bikes against the cobbler statue again and went into the bakery. They were just bringing out a tray of hot glazed doughnuts from the back. I bought one for me

and two for Georgie. I love glazed doughnuts. I know that they're junk food, but I'm just a kid, so I get to eat junk food sometimes. My mother and father *never* eat junk food. And Granpa says he intends to die without ever eating at a McDonald's. He says he wants that written on his tombstone.

By the way, Georgie and I did a terrific presentation in fifth grade about junk food. It has nothing to do with this story, but it was so cool that I put it on my website. You have my permission to use it if you have to do an oral presentation at your school. But make sure you tell your teacher that it comes from Cheesie Mack. Otherwise, it's cheating . . . and, as I said, I hate cheating.

We were just finishing our doughnuts when the inside of the coin store lit up and a man unlocked the front door. I wiped my sticky hands on my socks. Georgie licked each of his fingers, wiped his hands on my pants, and grinned. I smacked him, and we went into the coin store.

It was a different man from the bookkeeper guy we'd spoken to the night before. I handed him the two pieces of the receipt. "We'd like to get our penny back."

The man looked at the receipt, then pushed his glasses back onto his forehead and took the small brown envelope out of a drawer. He spread a black cloth on the counter and carefully poured our penny onto it. "This is a very valuable coin."

"We know."

"Where'd you lads get it?"

"I found it in my basement," Georgie said.

The man put a magnifying glass thing on his eye and examined the coin very closely.

"Now, if you lads can prove to me that this coin was not stolen and that you have the authority to sell it— that's something I have to do when the seller is underage—I'd be interested. Would you like to sell it?"

I shook my head and looked at Georgie. He shook his, too.

"It's worth a lot of money." The man examined both sides of the coin. "In this condition—it shows modest wear and has a subtle scratch on the reverse—I could offer you . . ." He looked up at the ceiling, then back at the coin, then right at us. "Twenty-two hundred dollars."

Georgie and I fainted.

Of course I am completely joking about fainting. But I will tell you that Georgie and I were stunned. I don't think either of us could speak or breathe normally.

"Twenty-two hundred dollars?" I repeated.

"Holy moley oley," Georgie squeaked.

"Twenty-two hundred dollars? Why is it worth so much?" I asked.

Mr. Whelan (he told us his name) turned the coin onto the back side. That's what we call tails, but there is nothing that looks like a tail on the back side of a Lincoln cent. Then he handed his magnifier to me.

"Look on the bottom." I saw three tiny letters: *V.D.B.*

Mr. Whelan then explained, with lots of detail, what happened in 1909 and why it made our coin so

$$$$! ———————→

valuable. It would take about three chapters to write everything that Mr. Whelan told us, and I'm guessing you'd rather read about Ms. Prott and me and Georgie than three chapters about a man named Victor D. Brenner. So here comes a much shorter version.

In 1908, President Theodore Roosevelt decided that since 1909 would be the one hundredth anniversary of Abraham Lincoln's birth, it would be terrific to honor him by putting his face on a coin. But lots of people in the government hated the idea. Here's why:

1. Since 1861, one-cent coins had had the head of an Indian on them, and many people just didn't want to change. They thought that Indians were the symbol of America. But what's weird is that the woman who was the model for the head on Indian Head cents was the daughter of

a man who worked at the mint where they made the coins—and she wasn't the least bit Native American! I found this on the Internet.

2. No U.S. coin had ever had the image of a real person on it. Even George Washington refused to let the government put his head on a coin because he thought it was too much like what kings and emperors had always done.

3. The image of Abraham Lincoln that President Roosevelt wanted to use was sculpted by Victor D. Brenner, a Jewish immigrant from Lithuania, which is a cold little country bordering Russia. The U.S. Mint artists who had designed previous coins were jealous that he got the job and not them.

4. The U.S. Mint had started out 1909 by coining Indian Head cents. But President Roosevelt got his way, and they switched to Lincoln cents in May. Even though some

government people hated Lincoln Head cents, lots of everyday folks loved them, so when they were released to the public on August 2, 1909, long lines formed outside banks. Each person in line, many of them clever kids, was limited to one dollar's worth of coins. The kids resold the new coins, three for a nickel, making two cents' profit each time. Two cents might not sound like much to you, but in 1909, it was a lot of money.

Also, because Lincoln had freed the slaves, the new coins were especially popular among African Americans, who called them "emancipation money."

But on August 4, only two days after the coins were released to the public, the head of the U.S. Treasury found a way to get back at Victor D. Brenner. He said that people were upset because Brenner put his initials (VDB) on the back of the coin, so he stopped production and had Brenner's initials removed from the metal dies they used to stamp the coins. Brenner was insulted and very mad, but he couldn't do anything about it. Coins made after that had no initials on the reverse side.

Since both the Philadelphia and San Francisco mints produced one-cent coins, there were six different cents made in 1909. (There are pictures of all six on my website.)

The Indian Heads minted at the beginning of the year are worth a lot. The Lincoln cents with no VDB are not so valuable because there were millions and millions of them minted. But the Lincoln cents *with* the VDBs are really rare. And the 1909-S VDB, because there were only about 400,000 made, are the most valuable of all . . . by far.

When Mr. Whelan finished his story, Georgie immediately said, "We looked on the web, and a 1909, not San Francisco, without VDB is worth three dollars. Is that right?"

"Depends on the condition," Mr. Whelan said, "but that's a reasonable starting point."

"Do you have any of those you could sell?"

I had no idea what Georgie was doing.

Mr. Whelan searched through a drawer and pulled

out a small envelope. He laid it on the black velvet cloth next to our VDB coin. The envelope, which had a clear side, held a Lincoln cent and was labeled "1909 $3.50."

Georgie turned to me. "How much money do you have left?"

"Huh?"

"After you bought the doughnuts. How much?"

I looked in my pocket. "Three-seventeen."

Georgie looked at Mr. Whelan and pointed at the coin in the envelope. "Could we buy this coin for three dollars and seventeen cents?"

Mr. Whelan nodded.

"What're you doing?" I asked Georgie.

"Hold on a minute," Georgie said to Mr. Whelan, then grabbed my arm and pulled me outside. "I've got a plan," he told me. He was staring at me with a lot of determination in his eyes. "We cannot give that VDB coin to Mrs. Prott."

"Ms. Prott."

"Whatever." He put both hands in his hair and rubbed really hard, then took a big breath. "When we thought that penny was worth ninety-five dollars, and we planned to go to Six Flags, I was willing to give it up and lose a day at an amusement park. That was bad, but this is ridiculous! Twenty-two hundred dollars! I could go—*we* could go—to camp!"

He was right. It'd be enough. But even with my mind rattling with how much we love camp, I mumbled, "Her sister gave her the coin and died."

"Doesn't matter. Look, here's what we'll do. We buy that no-S, no-VDB coin for the money you've got. And that's the penny we give to Ms. Prott. She wants to remember the year her sister was born. She cares about the date, so we give her the 1909."

I gave him a long look. "It's stealing, Georgie."

"It is absolutely *not* stealing. She lost it. I found it. We could've just taken it directly to Mr. Whelan and sold it. And if we hadn't tried so hard to find her, she never would have seen that penny again. *Never!* Look at it this way, Cheesie. Any 1909 will make Mrs. Prott happy."

"*Ms.* Prott. And yeah, assuming she doesn't know it's supposed to be an S-VDB. Otherwise, she'll know we tried to cheat her." I paused to think, looking through the front window at Mr. Whelan, looking at the sky, looking at the almost-invisible fishhook scar on my thumb.

Finally I came up with a compromise. "Okay. What we do is not sell anything now. We take both coins. Then we give her the plain one. And then we see if she says anything. If she does, we give her the S-VDB."

"But—"

"You know I'm right, Georgie."

Ten minutes later we were back at Ms. Prott's. I had both coins in my backpack. In a few minutes we'd be going home with only one. Would we be rich or poor?

I picked up the artichoke knocker from the porch and tried to use it, but ended up rapping with my knuckles. Ms. Prott took a long time—no surprise!— to answer the door. She pointed us, with lots of smiles and fluttering hands, to a different room, a dining room.

Ms. Prott had been busy while we were gone. She

had prepared a snack. There were teacups and a plate of cookies on the dining room table. After showing us where to sit, she disappeared in slo-mo, and I looked around the room. Like her parlor, the dining room was full of old, worn-down stuff. The furniture, the rugs, the knickknacks on shelves . . . everything looked like the junk you see at yard sales. My teacup was chipped.

Georgie interrupted my investigation. "You looking for clues?"

I motioned for him to shush, then whispered, "Nope. Just noticing how poor she is. All this stuff . . ." I swung my arm around the room. "It's old and worn-out. Look at my cup."

Georgie nodded and shrugged at the same time. "How're you going to do this?"

"If she mentions the S-VDB penny, I'll just say, 'Oops! My mistake,' and give her the other one."

"Bad idea." Georgie started blinking his eyes very fast. "You're a terrible liar, Mr. Blinky-Boy. She'll know instantly. Better let me do it."

"What're you going to say?"

"The same thing. But I'll do it without flunking an eye lie-detector test."

We heard Ms. Prott coming, so I hurriedly dug out the two pennies and handed them to Georgie. He looked at them quickly, then stuck one in each front pocket, muttering, "VDB right, no VDB left. VDB right, no VDB left."

Of course, neither of us needed to hurry because it took a long time for Ms. Prott to come back from the kitchen or somewhere, pushing a rickety cart with a teapot on it. One of the wheels wobbled badly and looked like it was ready to come off.

"We brought your sister's penny," Georgie offered.

"Tea and cookies," she said with four smiles, two hand waves, and several head nods.

The cookies were small, very tasty, and there were a lot of them. But the tea was too hot to drink. That didn't bother Ms. Prott, though. She sipped it without even noticing that it was, IMO, molten lava. When she put her teacup down, Georgie mentioned the penny again, but maybe she didn't hear.

"How old are you boys?"

"I'll be eleven in August," I said. "Georgie's already eleven."

"I told you, didn't I, that I was ninety-six? I didn't bake these cookies. Good, aren't they? I used to bake, but I don't anymore. I don't do many things I used to."

A thought was bubbling up inside me. "Do you live here alone?"

"Oh my, yes. I've lived alone since my mother passed away."

Georgie started to reach into his left pocket, so I poked him and shook my head.

"And how do you do things like get your groceries and stuff?" I sipped my tea and ate my fifth cookie.

"Well, how kind of you to ask. The county has a service, and a very nice man comes around twice a week to deliver right to my back door."

"What if you need to go to the dentist or something like that?"

"The county sends a car to pick me up. But I rarely go to the dentist. I'm ninety-six years old, and I have all my teeth. I suspect that there aren't many my age who can say that!" She grinned. She did have nice teeth.

"And what if something in the house breaks?"

Georgie kicked me under the table and gave me a what're-you-doing look. I ignored him.

"In that case—and things do break, don't they?—I call a lady at the county. She finds someone to fix it for me."

I stood up and said, "Would you excuse me? I left something outside . . . on my bike . . . I mean *in* my bike . . . my bike's saddlebag thing." My eyes were blinking a lot. I could tell. I grabbed Georgie and dragged him outside.

"What the heck are you doing?"

"This lady is really poor," I said.

"So?"

"She has the county buy her food and drive her around and fix her toaster and all that stuff. She's really poor."

"So?"

"We cannot give her the bad penny."

"Oh no, Cheesie! We already decided."

"That was before we found out how poor she is. She needs the twenty-two hundred dollars."

Georgie spun around and pretended to bang his head against the side of the house.

"Come on, Georgie—"

"Yeah, yeah," he muttered to the side of the house. "You're gonna say, like always, 'Come on, Georgie, you know I'm right.'" He turned toward me, his voice getting louder. "Well, with twenty-two hundred dollars, I could go to camp! I do *not* know you're right!"

He reached in both pockets, took out the two pennies, and threw them at me.

"You do whatever you want!" Georgie ran to his bike and pedaled away.

I called after him, but he didn't look back.

Chapter 16
Cheesie Tells Everything

It's hard for me to write this chapter, but I'm going to try to put down everything exactly the way it happened, even though . . . Well, you'll see.

I watched Georgie get smaller and smaller until he disappeared around the corner, then I picked up the two pennies, sat on the top porch step, and felt terrible. The little kid I used to be wanted to cry, but I didn't. My chest was shaking like there was a sob trying to come out, but it didn't. I closed my eyes and hoped that when I opened them, Georgie would be riding back, but he wasn't.

Georgie is . . . Georgie was my best friend.

I don't know how long I sat there before I realized that Ms. Prott was in the doorway, staring at me. I took one more look down the block to where Georgie had disappeared, then stood up. She held the door open. I walked back in. We moved very slowly toward the parlor.

"Ms. Prott, I brought your penny back." I held out my hand. Both coins were in my palm. "And I brought another penny, too. This one"—I found the S-VDB and held it out in my right hand—"is the one your sister put in the envelope. It's very valuable."

She nodded and took the coin.

"This one"—I held out the no-S-VDB coin in my other hand—"has the same date, but it's different, and it's worth much, much less."

She looked back and forth from the coin in my hand to the one in hers.

My eyes got watery. "They are both as old as your sister, and like your sister said, they'll never die. You can sell the valuable one and—"

Quit it! I said to myself, but it was too late. I plopped down on a sofa and felt tears on my cheeks.

Ms. Prott sat down next to me. She didn't say anything for a very long time. "I've been alive almost a

century. I taught high school. I was a nurse in the war." She handed me the tissues and touched my hand. "I've rid‑

den on an elephant. And I've flown in a hot‑air balloon. I'm old and frail, but I'm a good listener. Would you like to tell me what's wrong?"

So I told her everything. My words jumbled out so fast that she had to squint to keep up. But she listened silently. Her many quick movements disappeared. There was no fluttering or head nodding. She didn't even smile. When I told her about Georgie's not going to camp and me staying home to be with my best friend, she asked which camp and where it was. And when I told her that at first we were going to keep the S‑VDB penny and give her the other one, but that I changed my mind once I realized that her house and stuff were old and that she needed the money, she smiled a little bit.

I took a deep breath, plunked my head against the back of the sofa, wiped the last wetness out of my eyes, and ended with, "It looks like this will be the worst summer of my life."

She nodded once, then thought for a long time. Finally she asked, "How did you determine that the Lincoln Head cent was worth twenty-two hundred dollars?"

I had stopped crying. "There's this coin store on Main Street."

"That was very clever of you. Did you talk to Mr. Whelan?"

How did she know? I nodded.

"Do your friends call you Ronald?"

"Cheesie," I said softly. "Everyone calls me Cheesie."

"Cheesie it is." She picked up a small book next to a telephone on the table next to her, looked in it, and then dialed a number. "Mr. Whelan? Yes. This is Glenora Jean Prott. Very well, thank you. Yes." She looked at me. "I shall be sending a lad, Mr. Ronald Cheesie Mack, down to you with a coin I wish to sell. Give me your best price and credit my account. Yes, he'll be along shortly." She hung up the phone and turned to me. "Cheesie, I am a numismatist. Do you know what that means?"

I nodded. "A coin collector."

She took a scrapbook sort of thing off a shelf next to her and put it in my lap. There were about ten other books just like it on the shelf. She opened it. It was a collection of Lincoln Head cents with every hole filled.

"My sister sent me that coin for two reasons. I told you only the emotional one. The other reason was that I needed it to complete my collection. When I lost it, I purchased another to replace it." She pointed at a coin with "1909-S VDB" printed under it, then held the one we found right next to it.

"But I think I'd prefer the coin my sister sent me." She removed the 1909-S VDB coin from her coin book and replaced it with the one from Georgie's basement.

She reached for my hand and put the penny from

the coin book in my palm next to the three-dollar coin. Her skin was thin and dry and very soft.

"You did a very good thing today, Mr. Cheesie Mack. Now, do me a favor and take that coin to Mr. Whelan, and then go find Mr. Sinkoff and convince him to be friends again."

I shook my head. "He's too mad at me."

"That will change sooner than you think."

I shook my head harder.

Her on-off-on-off smile returned and she nodded her head several times. "Best friends are forever. I am convinced of it."

She walked with me to the front door. I was so depressed that without even trying, I walked just as slowly as she did. As she opened the door, she put a hand on my shoulder. "There's one thing more, Mr. Cheesie Mack. I am not poor. Actually, I am quite rich. My mother left me this home and quite an ample sum of money that I have wisely invested. You needn't worry about me."

Then she gave me a hug. She smelled like baby powder and flowers.

I walked outside, stuck the coins in my pocket, and trudged to my bike. I had left it plopped on the sidewalk, but someone had picked it up and propped it against the fence.

"Cheesie?"

I turned around. Georgie was straddling his bike.

"How's it going?" he asked.

I didn't know what to say. "Okay, I guess."

There was a long pause. I didn't look at Georgie, and I'm pretty sure he wasn't looking at me. Finally he said, "Umm, did you give her the penny?"

"Uh-huh. She had another just like it. She wants me to sell that one for her."

There was another long pause. There didn't seem to be anything else for either of us to say.

Georgie broke the silence. "Yeah, well, I've been riding around thinking, and I think you were right and I was wrong, and I'm sorry I made fun of how much your ears stick out."

"You didn't make fun of my ears."

"I know, but I thought about them." He reached out and flicked my ear and grinned.

I grinned back, and we rode to Mr. Whelan's and gave him the coin, and we were best friends again. Maybe, like Ms. Prott said, "forever."

On the way home, I told Georgie everything that happened while I was inside The Toad.

(I've changed my mind. Even though it's Ms. Prott's house and not haunted, it still seems like The Toad to me.)

He was really surprised when I told him that Ms. Prott was rich.

"Look, I apologized and I meant it, but I think it stinks that she didn't give us even a tiny reward."

I hadn't thought of that. "We still have the other coin as a souvenir."

"Yippee. It's worth three bucks. Big shmeal."

"We did the right thing, Georgie."

He shrugged. "I know. But I can still be a little bit angry."

I gave him a super-stern look. "If you're angry, I'm irritated."

"If you're irritated, I'm aggravated."

"If you're aggravated, I'm infuriated."

"If you're infuriated, I'm transpaxulated," Georgie said.

I smiled and gave Georgie a thumbs-up sign. This is another game he and I play. The rule is that you have to use a bigger or harder word each time. Since I have a larger vocabulary, Georgie mostly wins the game by making up a super-big word.

(There's a word game kind of like this on my website.)

When we got back to my house for lunch, Goon was reading a book, Granpa was watching golf on TV (he has never played, but he thinks he knows exactly what the players should do at each hole), and Mom was in Dad's office doing something with his computer. I made BLART sandwiches for Georgie and me, and a BLT for Mom. I was feeling so good, I even made a sandwich for Goon. Granpa likes to make his own lunch.

While I was pouring drinks, I had an idea. "Georgie, let's build a tree house this summer."

"We did that two summers ago."

"That was just some planks nailed to a branch, and

it was only ten feet up. I'm talking about walls and a roof and building it in the tree outside your attic window with an extension cord for electricity. We could rig up a pulley to get the boards and stuff up there. And nail about thirty boards onto the trunk to make a ladder."

It was a great plan. We were both grinning when I set Goon's sandwich down next to her.

"What's this?" she asked.

"A LART sandwich."

"For what?"

"For you."

"Why?"

"Just because."

"Don't expect me to make one for you tomorrow just because."

I shrugged and walked away.

"But thanks anyway," Goon said to my back as I carried Mom's sandwich into Dad's office.

Georgie took a bite of his BLART while he was following me and had to pull his plate up to his face to catch the drippiness that glorped out on his face and everywhere else. "For that tree house, my dad has some old rug pieces in the garage," he said. "We could nail those down and bring up sleeping bags and my TV and play video—" He didn't finish his sentence because he took another super-dribbly bite.

Mom seemed very frustrated with her computer stuff.

"I wish your father kept better track of the checks he writes. Hey, thanks for the sandwich." She took a bite. "How did it go with the lady you were helping?"

"Huh?"

"You had to return an envelope?"

"Oh, that. Fine."

"Actually, she called a little while ago. Found our number in the book. She'd like you boys to do some yard work this weekend."

"Yard work?"

"Sure. Cut the grass, weeding . . . jobs like that."

Georgie looked confused. I am completely sure that I did, too.

"You are helping her, aren't you? Ms. Prott, right?" Mom continued.

"Well, kind of, I guess. We were. I mean, we did."

"She'd like you to come over every week, starting this weekend. And in the winter, she'd like you to shovel her walks."

Georgie's lips and chin were white with ranch dressing. "Is she going to pay us for our slave labor?"

"Me too," I murbled into my sandwich.

Mom dipped her BLT into some of the ranch dressing on my plate and took a bite. "She is. In fact, she said she'd like to pay you for the whole next year in advance. And she understands that you won't be able to work during the summer when you two are away."

Both Georgie and I had sandwiches poised in midair. I had just taken a huge chomp, but I was too confused to chew.

"Away? Huh?" I grunted through the BLART bite.

"Ms. Prott told me what you boys did about that coin." Mom took another bite of her sandwich and made us wait while she chewed and chewed and finally swallowed. "I am so proud of you both. I've already told your father, Georgie. Ms. Prott has given you a reward. She's paid for your camp this summer!"

We screamed.

We jumped.

We dropped our sandwiches on the rug and made a huge BLART mess.

Mom didn't care.

The End

Chapter 17
After the Story Is Over

I lied.

About two million pages ago, I explained that I wrote Chapter 0 last. But then lots of things happened in the summer, so I am writing this chapter absolutely last.

I promise.

A chapter like this is called an epilogue, but that is not a word kids use very often. It means the place where you put the moral of the story or what happens after the story ends. So here goes.

Three weeks after we dropped our sandwiches, two weeks after the pizza party, and one week after we did Ms. Prott's yard work—it was easy—Georgie and I were on the bus with all our old friends and a bunch of maybe new ones. We were out of Massachusetts, past New Hampshire, and on the Maine Turnpike heading north to what would become the greatest summer camp experience of our lives.

Here's what happened at camp:

1. Anticipation
2. Disaster
3. A Big Decision
4. Big Problems
5. Amazingly Great Fun
6. Huge Disaster that culminated (This is the last big word in this book. It means "ended.") in . . .
7. A Surprise Conclusion that even I was amazed at . . . and I was there!

It's all in my next book, which I'm going to begin writing immediately after I finish this epilogue and go to the bathroom. I haven't figured out what the title will be (because I haven't written the book yet), but by the time you read this, the title will be on my website.

This really is the last chapter of this book. If you liked it, please tell your friends because Mom says if lots of people buy my books:

1. I'll have enough money to pay for college on my own.
2. My parents can retire.
3. Mom can grow her hair long and do pottery like she always wanted to.
4. Dad might finally fix up his motorcycle (which has been broken in our basement since before I was born and has a totally excellent sidecar that I've never ridden in), so that he and Mom could travel together from Alaska to the bottom of South America before they get too old for their own adventures.

BTW, Mrs. Crespo convinced Georgie and Lana Shen to combine their pizza parties so no one would be left out, so with eighty dollars to spend, Georgie was able to have his pizza-eating contest after all, and Lana Shen tried to sit next to me, but I got a bellyache from eating too fast or something, so I sort of stood behind Georgie and watched him eat eight slices and win.

Double-BTW, Georgie and I did not build a tree house. We did not have time.

Triple-BTW, I never did figure out about the mysterious *Eureka* word. I think it had something to do with Eureka Avenue, but why was it dented into the paper that was wrapped around the 1909-S VDB Lincoln cent and the heart necklace? I guess I could ask Glenora Jean Prott, but I'd rather ask you. If you have a theory, please go to my website and tell me.

And that's what happened at the end of fifth grade.

So . . . finally . . . at last . . . and in conclusion, *Cheesie Mack Is Not a Genius or Anything* culminates with this epilogue.

This is the third-to-last sentence.

I hope you liked this book.

Go to my website.

Signed:

Ronald "Cheesie" Mack

Ronald "Cheesie" Mack (age 11 years . . . yesterday!*)
CheesieMack.com

The Very End
(but keep reading anyway)

*If you want to know about my birthday party (super cool and very different), go to the birthday page on my website. And if your birthday was super cool and very different, tell me about it.

This Is Not a Chapter.
Visit CheesieMack.com If . . .

1. You liked this book . . . or if you didn't . . . or whatever. (page 3)
2. You want to tell me your grandparent nicknames. (page 10)
3. You know any countries with money that doesn't break into hundredths. (page 26)
4. You have an idea what it will cost to mail a letter fifty years from now. (page 31)
5. You have an image of a cool stamp and a clever, weird, or funny caption to go with it. (page 31)
6. You know anything about frog and toad

leg lengths. (page 60)

17. You've got another way to determine if Glenora Jean Prott was a Ms. or a Mrs. (page 189)

18. You want to see my and Georgie's junk food presentation. (page 192)

19. You want to see pictures of the six pennies minted in 1909. (page 198)

20. You want to play my and Georgie's Bigger-Word game. (page 215)

21. You want to know the title of my next book. (page 221)

22. You know why *Eureka* was dented into the paper in the envelope. (page 224)

23. You want to know about my birthday or tell me about yours . . . or just say hi. I hope you do! (page 224)

Acknowledgments

While writing this book, Cheesie got a lot of guidance from two new best friends, agent Dan Lazar and editor Jim Thomas, and one best friend he's known all his life, author Julia Quinn. He is very grateful for their help.

STEVE COTLER

is a retired Little League catcher who's also been a shoe salesman, telecom scientist, singer-songwriter, *Apollo 1* computer programmer, Hollywood screenwriter, Harvard Business School MBA, investment banker, and door-to-door egg man. He lives with his wife and writes in Sonoma County in Northern California's wine country. He thinks he is and always will be eleven years old.

ADAM McCAULEY

has illustrated twenty-two children's books, including Jon Scieszka's Time Warp Trio series, Louis Sachar's Wayside School series, and Betty Hicks's Gym Shorts series. Adam also illustrates picture books, and his animation "Fast Food" is in the permanent new-media collection of SFMOMA. When he's not drawing, Adam enjoys cooking, playing drums, and surfing in the cold Pacific waters. You can see more of his work at AdamMcCauley.com.

Visit Cheesie online at CheesieMack.com.
Visit Steve at SteveCotler.com.